Alan Sillitoe

CW00358181

was born in 1928, and left school
various factories until becoming
assistant with the Ministry of Aircraft Production in 1945.

He enlisted in May 1946 into the RAFVR, and spent two
years on active service in Malaya as a wireless operator.
At the end of 1949 he was invalided out of the service
with a hundred per cent disability pension.

He began writing, and lived for six years in France and
Spain. His first stories were printed in the *Nottinghamshire
Weekly Guardian*. In 1958 *Saturday Night and Sunday
Morning* was published, and *The Loneliness of the Long
Distance Runner*, which won the Hawthornden Prize for
literature, came out the following year. Both these books
were made into films.

Further works include *Key to the Door*, *The Ragman's
Daughter* and *The General* (both also filmed), the *William
Posters* trilogy, *A Start in Life*, *Raw Material*, *The
Widower's Son* – as well as eight volumes of poetry, and
Nottinghamshire, for which his son David took the
photographs. His latest novels include *The Open Door*,
Last Loves and *Snowstop*. With his wife, the poet Ruth
Fainlight, he divides his time between London and a
house in France.

By the same author

ALAN SILLITOE

Leonard's War

A Love Story

Flamingo
An Imprint of HarperCollins*Publishers*

Flamingo
An Imprint of HarperCollins*Publishers*
77–85 Fulham Palace Road,
Hammersmith, London W6 8JB

Published by Flamingo 1993
9 8 7 6 5 4 3 2 1

First published in Great Britain by
HarperCollins*Publishers* 1991

Copyright © Alan Sillitoe 1991

The Author asserts the moral right to
be identified as the author of this work

Author photograph by Brett Hambling

ISBN 0 586 09232 3

Set in Sabon

Printed in Great Britain by
HarperCollinsManufacturing Glasgow

All rights reserved. No part of this publication may be
reproduced, stored in a retrieval system, or transmitted,
in any form or by any means, electronic, mechanical,
photocopying, recording or otherwise, without the prior
permission of the publishers.

This book is sold subject to the condition that it shall not,
by way of trade or otherwise, be lent, re-sold, hired out or
otherwise circulated without the publisher's prior consent
in any form of binding or cover other than that in which it
is published and without a similar condition including this
condition being imposed on the subsequent purchaser.

Part 1

ONE

The straight road going inland from the coast was shaded by giant plane trees. Then it looped into a wooded col for some kilometres before descending into Bedarieux. Looking along the main street, the hills seemed close. In summer they held in the heat, and in winter sent down the rawest cold. They made the streets appear narrower than they were, but on a summer's day we were drawn towards a book fair by folksongs crowing from loudspeakers. Steps led beyond the dozen stalls to the classical-style town hall with, squarely along the façade, the usual logo of LIBERTÉ, EGALITÉ, FRATERNITÉ.

In 1940 soldiers back from France were billeted in the warehouse of a Nottingham suburb. Many sat on the pavements, relaxing after their ordeal, their strained eyes unable to refute the happiness of being in England. As kids we scrounged the foreign coins from their pockets, and while I read those words which even now bring a response from both heart and reason, one of the soldiers began telling us how he had seen (or maybe only heard about) Maurice Chevalier performing by the roadside as hundreds of refugees went by. Destitute, he hoped to gain a little money before going on his way. Another swaddie said that Maurice Chevalier had been killed by a German plane machine-gunning up and down the road near Dunkirk.

When I told the story to my father he said that all soldiers were notorious romancers and must have been pulling my leg, because he hadn't heard such news on the wireless or read about it in the *Evening Post*. I argued that we would know soon enough that it was true, though we never did, and so I had my first lesson in the effect of rumour on the imagination, such a scene of death and devastation creating a livelier picture if a famous person like Maurice Chevalier was put into it.

A book fair, however modest, reinforced the cultural atmosphere of the town, volumes of poetry and local history spread out

7

for people to inspect and buy. A hundred years ago Bedarieux was a place of forges and glassworks, with coalmines in surrounding villages, till the owners, unable or unwilling to pay proper wages to their employees, closed the factories. The population of the area fell by half, but its manufacturing past remains in various small ventures, while the socialist council puts on a book fair to give more animation to the town.

At one of the stalls we met an English photographer friend, who introduced us to the organiser of the festival, and he invited us to a celebratory lunch in the station dining room. It took two hours to go through the courses, and towards the end the atmosphere was so close that we went out for some fresh air.

The sun at its zenith gave little shade, and there was no cooling wind. I opened the flap of my haversack-cum-mapcase to make sure there were some cigars to offer when coffee was brought in. On the outside, over which the flap fell and fastened, were compartments for pencils, pens, and perhaps a protractor. There were also six sockets, like those of a bandolier, into which I inserted ink cartridges.

Why the revelation took place only on this occasion is hard to say, but the serious forlorn face of Leonard Frankland, a life-long shunter on the railway, appeared as if he had actually followed me to southern France, and expected me to greet him with: 'Hello, Leonard, how have you been all these years?'

His favourite stage show, put on at the local theatre during the nineteen-thirties, had been *The Chocolate Soldier*, and I recalled his amusement at the hero of the play using his bandolier not for lethal ammunition but for sticks of chocolate, a commodity far more useful to a fighting man in a tricky corner. Leonard appreciated the joke because he had served in a county regiment during the Great War, a conflict which seemed closer to him now that he had reached middle age than not long after the experience itself.

At the table I scribbled a few lines – at the risk of offending our hosts – as a reminder to write his book, details heard from different people during and since the years in which the events took place. One could not commemorate Leonard Frankland with less and, spiralled back from the heat of Bedarieux to the haze of a Midlands city, I began to write an account of his War.

HEADLINES I

SOVIET-GERMAN NON-AGGRESSION PACT.

BRITISH GUARANTEE TO POLAND.

PRESIDENT ROOSEVELT APPEALS TO HITLER.

POPE BROADCASTS AN APPEAL FOR PEACE.

SPECIAL SESSION OF UK PARLIAMENT.

MR CHAMBERLAIN'S STATEMENT.

TWO

They set their tokens on upcoming numbers hoping to rake in a few quid for the price of a threepenny card.

Legs Eleven – Sophie looked down.

Key to the Door – So did Leonard, sheltered by the fumes of pipe and fag smoke, and the hop-like odour of beer.

Number Ten – you'll never live there.

Bed and Breakfast – At two-and-sixpence she'd had it often, but kept the fact as close as possible to herself.

Clicketty-click – the lick of the beast. She'd had that a few times as well.

So on through the gamut, some hearts slow but mostly fast.

Thirty-nine – O gone forever! – for many but not for her.

Kelly's Eye – For me myself and nobody else.

Fifty-four – the pick of the sheets.

'Housey!' Her scream was a claymore cutting the fug. 'I've won! I've bleddy won!'

Doubting Leonard double-checked and then, hand high, she got her winnings, to groans from those who hadn't and never would, a woman shouting nevertheless 'Good old Sophie!' of a lovely big white five-pound note, and a cabbage-coloured quid as well.

She clicked her large black handbag shut. 'I've never won owt before. I'll bet I've spent a fortune all these years, and now I've got summat back.' Eyes glazed with pleasure, she turned to Leonard. 'The excitement's made me want to pee, duck. I'll bring you a pint, though, on the way back. We can drink all we like tonight.'

Strange how his head had stopped aching as soon as she came to the table. He hoped he would be able to see her again, for she was lucky, and generous, and had a wonderful laugh, as if she didn't care for anybody in the world, which couldn't be so, because hadn't she mentioned taking toffees and comics home to her children?

THREE

Sam was eighteen and, having been a long time in the Boys' Brigade (brisk, with a short haircut, a pillbox hat, and believing in all it stood for if nothing else), told his father he was going to sign on for seven-and-five with the Royal Marines. Leonard asked him not to. Only last night he had dreamed he was back on the Somme. 'I know what it's like.'

'You don't.' Sam flipped the coloured pages of a small atlas and gazetteer he usually browsed through more slowly. 'It'll be different this time.' He had tried to track Allan Quatermain and Captain Goode in Africa so as to make the adventurers more real as people. He had read *The Lost World* and *She* and *With Clive in India* and *Treasure Island* and *Martin Rattler* and *Sanders of the River* – the localities where they travelled more immediate than his own while reading them. A range of mountains, dark blue against the sky, that you had to go through jungle to reach, and after that was a vast desert to cross. When he left the Marines he would explore some far-off part of the British Empire, and only come back when he was rich. 'Anyway, you was in the army, not the Marines. That's different. And when you told me all about the Great War, you said you liked it, didn't you?'

Leonard couldn't help but laugh. 'I always said it was dreadful, as well. And don't forget that your Uncle Jack was killed.' You didn't want to harrow young minds, and even if you did try to put them wise on the long and the short of it you couldn't get anywhere near the truth. 'What about your job at the Co-op? Mr Baker said they would be teaching you to drive a van soon.'

He shifted in his chair, dark eyes moist with determination. 'I want to join up more than I've ever wanted anything in my life.'

His son's eyes connived with innocence at the onset of any perils, and though Leonard wondered how it was that he had failed to pass on the right ideas, he recalled saying such things to his own father. He had broken an apprenticeship to follow the band into the last war, but his habit of vigilance, second nature from the shunting yards, saved him many a time from injury or death in the trenches. That, and luck.

'One careless move in the sidings,' he had told Sam, 'and you might not only get yourself killed, but somebody else as well. And they're the ones you have to think about.'

Many other cautionary words had been dealt out concerning what Leonard called The Battle of Life, a fight he had concluded to be far easier than the Lord's great battles which he had undergone in the war – until Beryl had died. 'If you must go, then I suppose you must, only for God's sake take good care of yourself.'

Sam smiled at a schoolbook picture showing T. E. Lawrence behind a machine-gun shooting at a train in the desert. 'I'll try, Dad.'

Another war in the offing meant he would be called up anyway, Leonard reasoned, and if his own luck in warfare ran in the family Sam would come through unscathed.

FOUR

Leonard was a sparely built man just over middle height. At forty-six his quiff of hair was grey, above a creased forehead that gave an aspect of permanent worry. This might have been due to the suffering in his life, though he would have had such marks anyway, lines made more distinct by continual alertness during work. He laughed so infrequently that when he did his pale blue eyes turned almost watery, a glint over which he had little control. *The Chocolate Soldier* swayed him from humour towards the inventive when he thought an even better equipped warrior would also have had small bottles of beer swinging from his belt like grenades. Beryl laughed more at his hilarity than at what was on stage, though it was the last time she did, because in six months the TB she'd had for so long killed her at last.

He nursed her, read books from the library, a chapter each night, as if wanting to see how the tale ended would keep her from dying. He took the wireless from the kitchen and installed it by her bed, sat all hours with her when not at work or shopping or cooking or cleaning the house or making sure the children got off to school on time. At night he slept by her side on a camp bed, believing that with faith and unremitting attention she would be with him in old age. 'You'll see me out,' he laughed, when she couldn't sleep one night because she thought she was going to die. 'I'll be the first to go, you can bet on that.'

She looked at him, holding back breath so as to hide the fact that she had to struggle for it. A pink light glowed through her tissue-paper skin, and as the lantern of her spirit faded it took his hope away. When he asked the doctor if she could be sent to a sanatorium he was told she would be better off at home. Leonard knew what that meant, and so did she.

The straitjacket of work at the shunting yards stopped him cutting his throat – that, and the fact that four children had to be seen to. He might also have taken to drink, but only on the odd evening a week did he sit for as long as a pint lasted, hoping to win a few pounds at housey-housey for down payment on a set of *Practical Knowledge For All* which he had promised Paul, who was still at school.

Such speculation was brutally pushed aside by worry about Ivy who, at seventeen, was nearly as thin as her mother had been. Lately she had lost appetite, and was riven by a cough that neither linctus nor cosseting would cure. Serving in a shop exhausted her more than seemed reasonable, but when he told her she ought to see a doctor she wouldn't listen. You would if your mother was alive, but he didn't say that because her mother was dead, and to remind her of it, which she didn't need anyway, would make her even more afraid. Never a ready talker, she kept herself as solitary as possible in a house of five. As a child she was only lively on getting home from Sunday School, and several of the shelf of books were prizes she had been given.

Eunice was nineteen, healthy and vigorous, and greatly different in body, her teeth white and even, and features that glowed with a selfishness he sometimes found hard to accept. When he teased her about finding the right young man to marry she told him she wouldn't waste her time on any such thing. 'I've got other ideas. If it wasn't for this rotten war coming up I'd go to France for a holiday. Or some such place. Muriel at work went on a trip to Paris a couple of years ago with her mam and dad, and she says it was lovely.'

He smiled at the idea of going to France for pleasure, having been there himself and known parts of it he didn't care to see again. 'Maybe the war won't come, after all. That's what Chamberlain says. And if it does perhaps it'll be over by Christmas!'

She laughed at him trying to be funny. 'I'll go there, though, even if only on a day trip to Boulogne. I don't want to stay in this country all my life.' At fourteen she had gone to work in Boots' factory, had learned to type at night school, and was now in the office. She had worked up her Pitman's shorthand, and was waiting for a vacancy as a secretary. As little as sixpence a week had been saved since her first wages, and he knew she had enough in her Post Office bank book to spend ten pounds on a holiday in France.

When he said he had fallen for a woman called Sophie Waterall and was going to bring her home to live with them, her face coloured scarlet, as if the room in which the world turned had suddenly drawn its curtains on her. 'What do you mean? Another woman?'

'Another? You talk as if I'm the Sheik of Araby. I've only ever had your mother, and I'll love her till my dying day. But I got talking to this nice woman in a pub the other week, and we're very fond of each other. You forget how lonely life can be for me sometimes.'

You couldn't tell what Ivy on the other side of the fireplace thought, which he almost preferred, because he had never seen Eunice with such a hard expression.

'What's she like?'

He poked a spill between the bars to light his cigarette. 'I'll bring her and introduce her. I suppose it might be a good idea for you to get to know her beforehand.'

'We'll have to see about that.' She poured a cup of tea for her sister before serving him. The set of his mouth told her she wouldn't have much say in whether the woman lived there or not. And Leonard, disturbed by his own selfishness, was glad he would not have to argue the toss with Sam as well.

HEADLINES II

ANGLO-POLISH ALLIANCE SIGNED.

FINAL BRITISH NOTE.

GERMANS INVADE POLAND.

BRITISH AND FRENCH DEMAND THAT GERMAN
TROOPS BE WITHDRAWN.

EVACUATION OF CHILDREN FROM BRITISH CITIES.

FIVE

Sophie stood in the doorway of the living-kitchen, tall and verging on stout, open brown coat with a wide collar and large buttons, suggesting the sort of figure that made Eunice wonder if she wasn't pregnant, or 'on the tub' as people where *she* no doubt came from would say. It was also hard to decide whether she was timid, or merely weighing her chances of survival against Eunice who sat by the fireplace, Ivy drinking a cup of tea on the corner settle, and eleven-year-old Paul who was annoyed because his father had broken away from the game of draughts to say hello to this strange woman whose wavy brown hair showed when she took off her hat. The one thing all of them were sure about was that they disliked her and always would, so her stance confirmed that she was right to hesitate, though such perception on her part only heightened their silence.

Leonard told her to come right in, but when she sat down she wouldn't take off her coat. 'I've also got children,' he had said in the pub, 'but only three of them are at home.' It didn't matter, she told him, thinking that any kids of such a nice chap would be a pleasure to live with, compared to her own. Now she saw how wrong she had been.

He gave her a cup of tea, fetching the best blue Crown Derby cup and saucer which, Ivy remembered, their mother had most liked, the last of a full service wedding present given before she was born.

He put in milk and sugar, and stirred it slowly, hoping his children's dislike of her would go away if he took no notice, though when he introduced them, none said anything, or stood up to shake hands. He hardly expected them to, though would have liked to see some of the manners he and Beryl had always been careful to teach.

'I can't go home.' She spoke in a warm yet anxious tone. 'Not to somebody who's chucked me out.'

Eunice tut-tutted, as if such misfortune could have nothing to do with her. In any case she looked the sort of woman who could be lying, who came from the kind of people that bawled curses at each other and slung pots about, who neglected their kids and boozed their money, and where a man would hit a woman and throw her into the street just because he felt like it, or because she had been carrying on with all and sundry and deserved it.

He didn't want her to go back. 'You're welcome here.'

'Is she?' said Eunice's rolling eyes.

Leonard was still in his working clothes, shirtsleeves folded neatly up white arms. He looked at his watch without taking in the time, not entirely calm, straightening the chain across his waistcoat. 'You won't have to go back.'

Knowing she wasn't wanted, she would have left if she'd had anywhere to go. 'I told myself that you would be good to me.'

He didn't know what he was being. 'You can stay, that's all I know.'

She drank the tea in three long swallows, Eunice's eyes caught by the motions of her pale throat. It was as plain as a pikestaff that she would stay whatever anybody said. She needed shelter, and this roof must seem as good as the next. It was impossible to tell whether the slant to Sophie's eyes marked her as able to take a joke, or showed how sly she was, but Eunice sensed it was just such an uncertainty that her father had fallen in love with, or whatever word he liked to put on it.

'I don't think he wants the kids, either.'

'How many have you got?' Ivy spoke for the first time, but Sophie didn't answer. They assumed, however, that their father knew the number.

Leonard hoped Sophie was testing him, but feeling so uncontrollably welcoming he could hardly draw his words back. 'Bring them here, if he throws them out.'

Eunice wondered if he hadn't gone soft in the head, or if there wasn't a full moon above the rooftops. She didn't want to hear any such thing, pushed between them on her way to the front room as Sophie put the cup carefully onto the table and sat down again. 'Charlie's like a kid,' she said. 'He only wants me for what he can get out of me. He's always been like that. And when I put my foot down, he chucks me out.'

Eunice fastened her coat. 'Our mother's not cold in her grave, and you've picked up with this, this –' Tart, fancywoman, *prostitute* . . . unable to release such words before her father. Even if they concerned somebody else she couldn't use them out loud, not like some of the common girls met before she had been allowed to work in the offices, and even there you met one or two rum ones. The world would go on doing what it had to whatever she said, tears of chagrin falling hot on her cheeks.

Leonard held Sophie's shoulder as she reached for the empty teacup, a gesture either to ask for more, or as if she too was about to weep but didn't want to sully the carpet with her tears. At which Leonard turned angrily to Eunice. 'It's over two years since Beryl died.'

'It's five minutes to me, and it always will be. She was my mother, don't forget.'

He was stricken in two, yet in one body he was a lighthouse glowing in a storm and strong against any waves. When his hand moved to stroke Sophie's neck she turned, lips more full, as if to kiss his forearm. 'I don't want to cause any trouble. I've done with all that. At least I hope so.'

Ivy, face colouring at such a quarrel in a former house of calm, observed leaves in the teacup to discover her fate. Who would she meet, where in the wide world would she go, would she ever get rich, when would she die? She didn't know where she belonged, mostly belonged nowhere, so something must happen sooner or later, and what was happening now had nothing to do with her, but then, nothing ever had and never would, anywhere in the world.

Eunice drew a headscarf from her pocket. 'I'm not staying in this house, if *she* does. So you can tell me whether or not she is.'

The headscarf narrowed her face and made her, to Leonard standing before her, like judge and jury on his deepest wishes. 'Nobody tells me what I can and can't do in my own house.' He would never strike his children, but was damned if he would let them order him about. 'Do you hear what I say?'

'When are we going to finish this game, Dad?' Paul wondered

what the hell they were up to, keeping him out of all that was going on like this.

Leonard winked at Sophie, thought it lucky that when Charlie had thrown her out she had been wearing good clothes: a highnecked white blouse fastened by a gold brooch with a purple stone in the middle, a smart grey skirt and high-heeled shoes buttoned across the insteps. 'We'll cancel that round,' he said to his son, 'and have another match tomorrow. All right?'

Sophie's smile revealed to Ivy (and for a woman of over thirty she had lovely skin) a darkened tooth at the side of her mouth. Leonard helped her off with her coat as if she was the Duchess of Windsor, indicating that she had won the first round, a continuing smile showing Eunice that she would pull off all the others as well.

SIX

Eunice walked down St Ann's Well Road in the drizzly summer rain knowing that her father had lost his will, and therefore his reason. He had no mind left, so his children (and she no longer counted herself one of those) might just as well not exist for all he knew or cared. She couldn't live in a house like that.

Muriel, her friend at the office, had a flat in West Bridgford and was a bit spinsterish in her moods and looks. Three years ago she had gone to church to marry John Sawtry, who worked in a shop in town. Not exactly tall, dark and handsome, but he had thick black hair and a thin swarthy face, and was a quart pot of goodness and consideration all through their courtship. Bridesmaids were waiting, and so was everyone else, and a reception had been booked at Marsden's Café. Muriel was about to make a change in her life which she didn't know whether she wanted or not, but didn't fancy getting left on the shelf at twenty-five.

John Sawtry hadn't turned up, just hadn't come, sent no message, gave no sign that he would let such a thing happen, and was never heard from again. He had either joined the Navy, gone on the tramp, or killed himself in a lonely wood. She no longer cared, and if by any chance she ever set eyes on him again – she swore to Eunice – she would pass him in the street without a word. That was the end of men for her.

'That's not what I'd do,' Eunice said, highly flushed at the injustice. 'If it had happened to me, and I saw him, I'd let him have it. I'd at least knock his block off.'

'Well, I'm not like that,' Muriel said, though they had a good laugh. At the same talk she told Eunice that she could share the flat if she paid her way. There was an inside bathroom and toilet, which pleased Eunice more than anything else, because she wouldn't have to go across the backyard in view of all the neighbours, and get whitewash on her skirt whenever she sat down to pee. At Muriel's flat she could lock her own door if she wanted, and from the window of her room have a sight of fields and the corner of a spinney.

Next morning, before Sophie and her father were out of their bed, she put her belongings into a case and two carrier bags. On the way to the bus a cheerful workman walked by her side asking if he could help in her struggle, but she looked daggers till he left her alone.

HEADLINES III

ENGLAND AND FRANCE AT WAR WITH GERMANY.

BRITISH EXPEDITIONARY FORCE MOVING TO FRANCE.

CZECH ARMY FORMED IN FRANCE.

CANADA DECLARES WAR ON GERMANY.

SOVIET TROOPS ENTER EASTERN POLAND.

AIRCRAFT CARRIER *COURAGEOUS* TORPEDOED OFF
IRELAND.

WARSAW SURRENDERS.

SEVEN

A line of green Corporation doubledecker buses stood along the pavement by the school railings. Sophie couldn't spot her own children in the hundreds there, but was glad she wasn't too late to see them off. Charlie must have sent them early, glad to be shut of them, because that bone-idle swine would never think to come and say goodbye.

She pushed her way through, bossy women calling the kids into order, and staring at her as if she had gone crackers. Just because she was where she shouldn't be. They were shouting and blowing whistles, when a sheepdog might have done the whole thing quieter. But then, these posh whores always liked you to hear what they was doing.

When she asked one of them where the kids were being sent she was told that nobody knew, but they would go somewhere safe from the bombing, you could be sure of that. 'I'm the mother of three of 'em,' she said, 'so you'd better let me bleeding well know.'

The woman flushed at Sophie's violent request, then smiled, but not too much in case her face cracked. 'You'll find out where when you see what bus they get into.'

'Thanks, duck. You're a lot of help.' The trouble was, the little sods could be anywhere in this mad crush. There would have been four of them if poor Clarence hadn't got run over, but she hadn't time to think about him now. She saw Norma's red gingernut in the crowd, and after pushing through two more lines of kids, smacked her ringingly across the face and grabbed her by the wrist. 'Where is Gilbert and Harry, then? I told you to look after them, didn't I, you spoilt little madam!'

'Right behind me, you daft prat.' Norma knew it was safe to swear at her mother, who only ever hit her when there seemed no reason to. Each of them had a carrier bag – Harry's already torn and clutched in his arms like a teddy bear – as well as a battered gasmask box slung over their shoulders. 'Here's a shilling each, now look sharp and get on that bus or it'll go without you.'

'Aren't you coming with us, Mam?' Harry said.

She glanced at the front of the bus and read the sign: Ashfield. 'Not on your life.'

He began to cry, and Norma thumped him between the shoulders. 'Shurrup. We're going to a big posh house where there's lots to eat, and bags of toffees on the floors. We'll have our own bed to sleep in, as well.'

'Move along there, come on, move along,' the bossy voice shouted, 'or you won't find a seat.'

'I don't want a bed all to myself,' Harry shouted.

'I do,' Gilbert said. 'It'll be like a tent. Anyway, if we stay here we'll get bombed.'

Norma found places for them on the bus, and looked out of the window at Sophie. 'I feel sick already.'

'You behave yourselves where you're going.' She was too excited at their adventure to cry, or even to worry. They were bound to be looked after better than if they stayed at home. 'If you don't, I shall hear all about it, and then you'll get my fist.'

'Even the smell of the seats makes me want to spew.' Norma's face was greenish as the bus jerked away in a cloud of diesel fumes. Others were already floating towards Castle Boulevard, some of the kids singing *There'll always be an England* . . .

'You'd think they were off to the seaside,' Sophie said, her hand back from a cursory wave.

'That's where I told mine they was going,' a man laughed, 'and it kept the boggers quiet, any road up.' He was dressed in a suit and wore a tie even at this time of the morning, had polished shoes and short grey hair well parted, the smart and knowing sort she could take a fancy to. But she loved Leonard, she told herself, hoping it was true, because whatever he did for her he wanted nothing back. He did it because he liked her, and had a good heart, and said he loved her – the bleddy fool. How could she think much of anybody who said they loved someone like her? It was a fact that she liked him back, but he was so nice that you had to.

'I wouldn't mind going on the bus with them.' It reminded her of trips in the country they had been taken on from school, and she felt alone for the first time. 'I wonder when I shall see them again?'

'Not until after the Duration, I expect.'

'How long will that be, though?'

'The last one was four years, so you'd better double it for this one, at least.'

In that time they would all be grown up, and she would be an old woman. She lit a cigarette to steady herself. 'You don't know what you're talking about.'

He put a hand on her arm, as if he knew better. 'Have it your way, missis. But if you're going to be lonely now they've been packed off why don't you come back to my house with me? I've got a few bottles of stout in the cupboard.'

'You've got a bleddy cheek.' She thought he hadn't come to see his kids off at all, but only to click with somebody.

He looked close at her, and smiled. 'You don't get much in this world if you don't ask, do you?'

She laughed, knowing he was right. 'That's what they all say. But I've got a husband to go back to.' She walked down the street, thinking that she hadn't much to give Leonard either, and that it would have been nice all the same to go off for an hour or two and have a drink of stout afterwards.

When they were in bed that night Leonard thought the reason she was being more passionate than usual was because she had said goodbye to her children. But whatever it was, he felt as if he had never been young before.

HEADLINES IV

BOMB IN MUNICH BEER CELLAR AFTER
HITLER'S DEPARTURE.

HM DESTROYER *BLANCHE* SUNK.

MARTIAL LAW IN PRAGUE. MANY STUDENTS SHOT.

GERMAN MAGNETIC MINES SOWN FROM THE AIR.

HM DESTROYER *GIPSY* LOST.

RAWALPINDI SUNK BY *SCHARNHORST*
AND *GNEISENAU*

RUSSIA INVADES FINLAND.

EIGHT

Leonard took the silver-framed photograph of Beryl off the mantelshelf and scissored it down to size so that it would fit into his wallet. It seemed only right, after Sophie came into the house. He could look at it in private whenever he wanted, and Sophie wouldn't have to try guessing who it was.

Then he rearranged the photographs of his parents, his brother Jack, and Sam his firstborn son, so that Beryl's absence wouldn't be noted. Paul looked on, and said nothing.

'It's so that I can carry your mother next to my heart,' Leonard explained, thinking him too young to understand.

He was left as always with the penance of Jack's loss, more acute since Beryl died, for he still saw himself as so responsible for his death that recalling Jack's face brought on a fainting weakness whenever he thought about him. Sometimes the eyes reproached him, as if Jack was in despair at not being able to get his own back, though at other times Jack's features seemed to laugh and call him a fool for imagining that anyone except himself could be responsible for his fate. Either way didn't ease Leonard's feelings, and alter the fact that he was the only one to blame. He sometimes wondered why he didn't take the photograph down, but he could not be a coward at facing up to what he had done.

Everything was chance, pure unfeeling chance, always had been and always would be. He had run to the colours in 1914, in time to go through the training and over the top at Loos, a battle which had turned into a bloodbath if ever there was one – the first of many. It was chance that he had survived, but by some fatal mix-up he had been listed with the dead, stated officially to be killed in action, and the error of a careless clerk or RAMC counter-of-corpses had caused the usual telegram to be sent to his parents.

Out of despair, foolhardiness, love or anger, Jack ran from the house unable to endure the terrible grief of his parents or tolerate the crushing onset of his own – as they drew the curtains to signify the disaster of Leonard's death to the street. It was exactly what Jack should not have done, but Jack loved his brother, wanted either revenge or to join him, not much caring if it turned out to be both.

The bitter accusation hurled at Leonard was that Jack need never have enlisted. Even later, after conscription started, he had a reserved job at the Royal Ordnance Factory and was considered too valuable to be wasted as cannon fodder. By the time the apologetic message came to tell them that Leonard was alive and not even wounded, Jack had taken the shilling and gone into camp, to be killed on the Somme the following year.

Their parents died within six months of each other, though waiting till 1920 to do so in case Jack turned up from the battlefields saying that a mistake had been made about him as well. Leonard knew it was hopeless, because Jack was one of the dead with no known grave. What else had they died of but broken hearts? Leonard had caused their grief, that was certain, fixing the reason for his own that would last forever.

Such thoughts were foolish, he knew it at odd moments, there were many similar stories in a war, yet he couldn't help telling himself that they were not. The anguish receded, but always came hauntingly back. That carefree wonderful walking out of work one sunny day, going home first to change into his best suit, and setting out with a gang of his pals, singing as they went down the street, to enlist – that had started it all.

He stared at the photograph of Jack in his khaki, a young, longish face with a moustache not heavy enough to hide the faint smile. Leonard felt his regret overshadowed by a keener dread at the resemblance to Jack of Sam his son, in spite of the fact that he also featured his mother. Beneath the joy of life dread could never be absent.

Now that Sophie lived with him sorrow for Jack had lost some of its pain, and hope for the absent turned into bearable optimism. His brother, his parents and his wife were no longer with him. Life must go on. He was happy, as even Jack would acknowledge he had a right to be, though Leonard knew that once responsible for your brother's death you would be accountable till the last breath was taken from you. Thus a few moments of thoughtlessness, locked into memory, must take a lifetime to pay for.

NINE

You would think the beer was going to run out, the way they mobbed the counter, but Leonard and Sophie found a table before the proper uproar set in. What else could you expect in The Rose of England?

They held hands and talked of old times and the new good times. Sophie didn't ask about his dead wife, and he never mentioned her absent husband. He had no particular wish to meet him, either, though he well knew that what you didn't like usually came to pass. But at the moment he was happy, and had felt a comparable lift of the spirit only on the steamer in mid-Channel when seeing France for the first time at the age of twenty as a soldier, all his friends around him, the nevertheless sad wheeze of a mouth-organ mellowing the warm breeze.

He also recalled that few of the battalion returned with him in 1919: forlorn, speechless, glum with hoping that one day they would hope again, otherwise empty. So he relished a vision of the happier departure, then corrected the game which his deceptive memory was playing, and remembered how he and a few companions had stood as close to the front of the ship as they could get, and actually cheered when they saw the cliffs at Folkestone. The older he got the more the yesterdays seemed like today, and the less he could remember with true clarity.

Yet nothing had been as wonderful as life now was with Sophie, because to be intimate with her was the kind of love he had imagined but hardly thought possible. Afterwards, he was at rest because they were at rest together. He whistled his way around the shunting yards in the day so that even his eternal vigilance was no longer the burden he now realised it had been. He only took in the fact that war had been declared when he said, 'Well, all I can say is I hope our Sam will be all right.'

'He will, duck. You shouldn't worry about it.' They sat in their usual corner after supper. 'That's what I've learned in life: not to let anything worry me. I don't need to now I've got you, though, do I?'

Her warm kiss on his cheek reinforced the notion of mutual comfort, and what could be better? He nodded, and smiled, but she was no longer close to him, leaning out of her seat and saying, 'That's him.'

He could hardly say in what direction the stab of her finger went, though caught the venom in her tone. 'Him? Who do you mean?'

'Charlie, my better half!'

Leonard did not turn. He could look, if he had to, when no one would notice, and a few seconds later, after a glimpse of the whole room, saw a tall thin athletic man of about forty with a lined and harrowed face, and greying curly hair, wearing a white scarf and holding a cigarette. Sophie's laugh was so loud that Charlie, who might not otherwise have seen her, fully taken up at the bar with his own piece of skirt, or so she judged her, looked with such accuracy in her direction at a sound that could only belong to one person in the city, that his gimlet eyes beamed straight to her face. It seemed to Leonard that this had been Sophie's intention, but he crushed the thought as unjust.

Charlie, whose *piece of skirt* Leonard saw in fact as a nice-looking young girl, showed no interest, and the crowded saloon soon blocked him from view. They went on talking about how much they loved each other, and would go on doing so forever, and what good times they would have – if not now, then after the war was over – until Leonard noticed a heightened excitement in her tone that had not been there before she had spotted Charlie. Having drained their glasses, and thinking it time to go home because he had to be early for work in the morning, he felt a tap at the shoulder, and even before looking knew who it was, heart floating endlessly between beat and beat, though he hadn't been five years a soldier for nothing, and could take care of himself.

Charlie's smile suggested the most heartfelt wishes. 'I hope you're going to be happy with her.' He had false teeth, a false heart, a false suit on his back, which together made a shine of real expression one might almost take to, a life of putting a cheerful face on a kind of purgatory he would never part with because any alternative would be worse in not letting him know who he was.

Yet Leonard felt some connection to Charlie, and didn't like it for placing him at a disadvantage. Charlie sensed this and, after a pause, which Leonard resisted filling, a more natural shade of malice crossed his features. 'She was a bleddy terror to me, but I'll tell you what, mate, you can have her, and you can have the kids as well, when they come back from wherever they are. I'm sure none of them's mine, anyway, so I'll never want the bleddy pests back.'

Leonard could understand a man feeling bad about losing a fine woman like Sophie – nothing to argue about there – but to disown your own children seemed the height of uncivilised behaviour. No wonder Sophie had packed him in, his eye said when he looked at her, but meeting only the blank needle-pointed grey tips that she turned on Charlie.

Having no more of it with that bastard, her lips tightened, losing their shape when she stood up and shouted full at his smiling phizzog for the whole pub to hear: 'You can clear off, you two-faced blinding get. If you don't, you'll get this pint glass between your eyes.'

The savagery of her threat was reduced, in Leonard's estimation, due to their glasses being in any case halves. Charlie's amusement lingered, as if the same thought had occurred to him, and he turned again to Leonard. 'I wanted to let you know what you were in for.' Then he went back into the crowd's safety, fearful of Sophie's wrath.

'And I'll let him know about you, you dirty bleeding ponce,' she screamed after him.

Such raging bad language could say no truth, and Leonard took her hand tenderly. 'Stop it, duck. You're with me now. You've got nothing to worry about.'

The rose flush stayed as if it were her normal colour. 'He wants to spoil everything good in my life. I can't tell you one half of what he's done to me. I sometimes wish I was dead, because if I was I'd be a lot better off, let me tell you.'

He was appalled at her slight regard for the power of his love to help, but saw how impossible it was at the moment to bring her back from such distant wastelands of blind anger. 'We won't come here again. We'll go to the Railway Man's Club. It's more respectable there. The beer's a few coppers cheaper as well.' Enthralled by his pity at her genuine pain, he lit cigarettes, and held the hand to stop the shaking when she put hers to her lips. 'You've got to calm down, and not let such things worry you.'

'I know,' she said. 'I try, but sometimes I can't.'

On the way home she stopped by a shop window and kissed him, not caring about people looking on, as if they were two youngsters of fourteen in the shade of a country lane – as he and his wife had once kissed, before he had asked her to marry him on getting back from France.

TEN

In the frosty dark of a winter's night, when even cats had abandoned the streets and entryways, a needle was stuck into the wood of a lintel half an inch from the glass. A length of cotton was threaded through the eye from which a button hung, and someone across the street concealed behind a wall pulled the cotton so that the button tapped rhythmically against the glass. Eventually the man or woman of the house came out to see who was there and found – Mr Nobody. Spirit-tapping was the game when they were kids.

Dozing by the fire after a long day, he dreamed he was again playing high jinks with a button as big as a head which may have been his own, and hearing kicks and thumps at the door knew it was too late for Guy Fawkes cadging, and in any case there was a blackout. It was also too early for Christmas carolling, though that was the sort of beggars the three of them seemed in the evening gloom when he opened the door. 'What do you want?'

Each held a carrier bag, and a gasmask in a box. They looked bedraggled and unearthly. 'Is Mam here?' the girl said, her face close up to his.

Charlie had kept Ted, the eldest boy, because he could go to work and bring money in, but the advent of this crew was something he hadn't looked forward to, though he had said nothing to Sophie, knowing that if they did turn up he would have to find a house with an extra bedroom. He couldn't say whether he didn't mention the problem to Sophie because it was gallantry not to, or because he didn't want to put her into a mood by interfering too much in her life.

They looked as if they had camped out on the rubbish tips for a fortnight, though they had obviously been fed well wherever they came from. When he led them through the scullery and into the kitchen Sophie glanced from the fire and said, as if they were the last kids in the world she wanted to see: 'I thought you lot had been evacuated?'

'We was,' Norma said, 'but they packed us off home.'

'We went to Dad's.' Gilbert, at nearly fourteen, had the same sharp face as his father. 'But he told us to come here.'

'How did he know where I lived?' Sophie wondered.

'He must have followed us from The Rose of England that night, when we were too wrapped up in each other to notice.'

'Yes,' she said to Leonard, 'he's a sly bleeder. I can just see him doing it.'

'We're clambed to death.' Norma drew a hand across her forehead. 'Is there owt to eat in the house?' At twelve she looked an about-to-be-grown-up Sophie, in the face though hardly yet in the figure. Harry at seven resembled neither of his parents, a thin-featured boy with blue eyes and tangled fair hair. Leonard set them on the sofa, and since Sophie made no move to help he asked Ivy to go into the scullery for some food and tea. 'Why did you come back?'

They glanced at each other, till Norma said: 'Gillie nicked stuff from a shop and got caught. The man nearly knocked his bleddy brains out. And our Harry broke a window with a stone.' She laughed. 'But you should have seen the people where we lived. They went crackers. So they gave us half a crown each and packed us off on the bus to come home.'

Gilbert screwed his hand into a piece of menacing stone. 'You're a liar. It's yo' who went thieving every day. She nicked some lipstick and powder from Woolworth's.'

'There won't be any more of that,' Leonard told them, 'if you're going to stay here.'

Sophie stood up as Ivy came in with a loaf and butter and set out the cups. Norma reached for the first cut slice of bread. 'I don't want to go back to that bleddy lot. We had to go to Sunday School, would you believe it? They was always on at us, the lousy sods. It was a rotten school, anyway. You got the strap every day if you said owt.'

'They only wanted to look after you properly.' Leonard took the bread back from Norma. 'You have to wait till you're served, in this house.'

She put out her tongue, but so quickly that Leonard didn't see, for which Ivy was glad, though maybe it would have been better if he had seen it, then in the ensuing ructions the mother as well as the children might have been chucked into the street and peace would have returned to the house.

Sophie wondered what tribulations they had been through, yet didn't feel like asking. They were still in one piece, and cheeky enough. 'Behave your bleddy selves,' she shouted, 'or Leonard will throw you out as well. You'll have to pull your socks up from now on if you want to stay here.'

They sat side by side, hands roped onto knees, a silence Leonard couldn't altogether trust. 'We didn't come on a bus,' Gilbert said. 'We spent the half-crowns on toffees. A man brought us on a lorry because Norma was nice to him.'

Whoever they had been evacuated with must have looked after them, because they wore decent clothes, the grime and tangle of hair not much older than the time taken to get here. 'Didn't they buy your tickets, and put you on the bus themselves?'

They looked at Leonard *gone-out*, Norma's shoe pressing against Harry's ankle. To get a true account of their adventures would be impossible. 'So you ran away?'

Norma leaned across to wipe Harry's nose with a rag. 'No, we bleddy didn't.'

'They're probably worried to death,' Leonard said.

'We did run away.' Harry's eyes shone at their enterprise. 'We talked about it in bed, when they couldn't hear us.'

'They'll be glad to get shut on us,' Norma said, 'the fucking religious bastards.'

Leonard's veins stood out in anger. 'Don't swear like that in this house. Ever again. Do you hear?' He recalled his mother's formula when he spoke words far less vile. 'Or you'll get your mouth washed out with carbolic soap.'

Norma parted her lips, but changed her mind, not sure of her ground. 'They must be going mad with worry,' Leonard said. 'I expect they went to tell the police because they don't know where you've got to. You shouldn't have run away.'

Sophie looked up from her seat of warmth. 'Oh, for God's sake leave the poor kids alone. Can't you see they're snatched and hungry?'

Norma went to her mother with a smile, eyeing Leonard with hatred as she kissed her hand. 'We are, Mam. Can we have summat to eat now?'

'The first thing they should do,' Leonard said, 'is pay a visit to the tap.'

Sophie gave them bread, and poured tea. She should never have let them go, and was double glad to see them back. There had been no bombing, and anyway they would be safe with her. She wouldn't let them go again, no matter what happened.

Half an hour ago, Leonard mused, they might as well have been in Australia, she had given them so little thought. It was pleasant to see her being the mother, but he wondered how he would be able to feed them on his wages, because surely their father, such as he was, wouldn't offer to do it. Still, he was working nights for a while, and that meant a bit extra.

HEADLINES V

RUSSIANS REACH MAIN KARELIAN DEFENCE LINE.

BATTLE OF RIVER PLATE. *AJAX, ACHILLES* AND *EXETER* DRIVE *GRAF SPEE* INTO MONTEVIDEO.

GRAF SPEE SCUTTLED.

CANADIAN TROOPS LAND IN BRITAIN.

INDIAN TROOPS LAND IN FRANCE.

RUSSIANS ADVANCE NORTH OF LAKE LADOGA.

ELEVEN

Drivers couldn't see more than a few feet in front and were trying to get out of town. When visibility seemed to increase they were so blinded by hope that an occasional vehicle mounted the pavement.

Hoar frost settling on their eyelashes, they tried to guide the drivers, but no one accepted their assistance, one cantankerous motorist bawling at them to bogger off, refusing even to wonder whether they could help or not. Norma ran to the back of his car and kicked the bumper, leaping into the fog like a wraith in a frock when he opened his door to hit her. Gilbert stamped on the running board and rattled the handle, the man calling that if they didn't stop their antics he would come out and punch their heads.

Failing as traffic police they wandered the streets of posher houses to do Christmas carolling, Harry piping 'Hark the Herald Angels Sing' through the flap of a letterbox. Cold gnawed painfully at their bodies, and Norma by the gate wrapped her arms around Paul to keep herself warm, till he pushed her away because it didn't seem right. Gilbert stood with Harry to get any money should a door be opened.

From not having two ha'pennies for a penny they pooled unexpected resources to buy a nelson square each, eating into the puddingy middles on the way to their common home a half-mile down the road towards town. Norma coughed on fog and oil fumes as they dodged stalled cars and buses. When Harry kicked a mudguard, angry after Gilbert had snatched the last of his nelson square, a man got out and chased them, but they vanished in four directions and met again in their own backyard.

Sophie and her kids had been thrown out by Charlie with little but the clothes on their backs, and not a stick of furniture to their names, so Leonard, with more population than he had bargained for, rented a bigger house on Thurland Street. He was in any case glad to leave the place in which Beryl had died, unable to live there too long with a woman he had fallen in love with in a pub.

His own tranklements weren't yet moved in, and between shifts in the marshalling yards he carried smaller items through the streets on his shoulders. Most of it was kitchen stuff – enabling them to mash tea and eat a decent meal – but also a box of books and some blankets. At the weekend he hired a handcart for a shilling, and cleared the previous place before Monday so as not to pay two lots of rent.

The house wasn't properly furnished on the upper floors, so the kids sat on worn planks dangerous with splinters, not daring to put on a light since there were no blackout curtains to draw. They had come in unbeknown to Leonard or Sophie who – Paul said, on getting back upstairs with a stump of candle – were in the kitchen smoking fags, supping tea, and holding hands. They wondered what they were doing that for.

'Just like the silly prats on the pictures,' Norma said.

Harry laughed, and flushed red. 'I'll bet they'll be fucking soon.'

Gilbert smacked him on the face, and when he began to cry Sophie called up for them to make less noise.

Paul sat on his own. His father didn't play draughts any more, and nobody else in the house could. The move and countermove of black and white enthralled him, fired his keenness in the art of tactics, hid him agreeably from all cares. When he pushed through his father's defences and got a king he thought his mother, glad at his success, smiled at him. Now he saw Sophie and his father in black and white, but could see no pattern in the way they behaved to each other.

He didn't feel he belonged to the house, with Dad and this woman, and her kids he had to be wary of all the time. He wanted to go back into the street and find that house which he and his father and Ivy really lived in. Even Eunice and Sam, who had always been on at him to be tidy, and forcing him out of the house in time for school, would have been more than welcome in the cosy circle. They were only camping in this one, until things got better. In the streets he would be on his own, but feeling lost and lonely, and wondering whether he would ever get there, wherever *there* was, threading the route and pondering on the set-up his father had taken on with no thought for anybody else – as he had heard Ivy say. But he had to stay where he was whether he liked it or not, though as soon as he could he would join up like Sam and get away from them all.

HEADLINES VI

GOERING TAKES CONTROL OF ALL GERMAN
WAR INDUSTRIES.

RUSSIAN 44TH DIVISION DESTROYED BY FINNS.

MR CHURCHILL BROADCASTS AN APPEAL TO
NEUTRAL COUNTRIES TO JOIN BRITAIN AND FRANCE
AGAINST GERMAN AGGRESSION.

HM DESTROYER *EXMOUTH* SUNK.

BRITISH PRISONERS RESCUED FROM GERMAN PRISON
SHIP *ALTMARK*.

TWELVE

Bacon, butter and sugar were rationed, so you didn't have to smile at the shopkeepers any more, Eunice and Muriel agreeing that fair shares for all seemed the only right thing in the world.

Instead of carrying buckets of coal from the backyard, or up out of a musty-smelling cellar, there was a clean gasfire, though they couldn't turn that on too often since it was so dear, but they locked and bolted the door after a day's work, or coming home with the shopping, and felt safe from the cold and everything else.

Eunice kept her own little fortress of jam and tea, bread and sugar and pressed ham separate on the kitchen table till one day Muriel said: 'We might as well put our stuff together in the cupboard, because we eat about the same and I'll bet it'll be cheaper.'

Muriel was slim and fair, with short hair, and Eunice liked her because she was so clean and neat. You couldn't always tell what she was thinking, but that didn't matter because then you didn't have to wonder what it was. Her greyish-green eyes looked at you like needles which didn't seem to be taking much in, and even if they were it wouldn't matter because she wasn't seeing anything anyway. Later Eunice found that she could be as lively and full of thought as herself.

They would put the gasfire on for half an hour, then keep it off for half an hour, then set it going again, and when they turned it off and it got cold it was time for bed. Both agreed that this was the best way because they shared the bills, and what money was left over was all the better for saving.

The only other occupant of the flat was a fat black and white cat that couldn't have kittens, and though Eunice didn't much like it it didn't matter because so far it only jumped on Muriel for a nightly cuddle. In any case Eunice had thought she would stay a few weeks and then look for a place of her own, but everything was so easy and comfortable that she didn't want to leave. Muriel talked to her about it. 'You might as well be here, as far as I'm concerned. We get on all right, and it makes it economical, both of us sharing.'

The temperature fell to freezing, some saying it was the worst winter on record. Wearing thick nightgowns they got into the same bed to keep warm. They took it in turns to make breakfast, and caught the same bus to work. At the canteen they ate a hot dinner at midday, and didn't need to cook anything at night, unless they boiled an egg or opened a tin of beans. Muriel saw to the food on Saturday, and Eunice cooked a shilling roast in the oven on Sunday. It was the best time of her life, she thought, except that now and again she went to see her father, though never stayed more than half an hour, with that Sophie and her mob of scruffy kids hanging around, waiting for a chance to rob her. It was as if she was visiting her father in prison, one that he had made for himself. She felt sorry most of all for Paul, who acted as if he had been dropped into the house from the sky, and didn't know how to escape his plight. He never said much. Sometimes she would give him a shilling, and he seemed grateful for that. But she didn't want him calling on her at the flat in case any of Sophie's kids came with him.

Every couple of weeks she went with Muriel to the library at the end of the road to change their books, because they often read for half an hour in the evening. Muriel brought Jack London and D. H. Lawrence and poetry books, but when Eunice tried them she couldn't make head or tail of it all because they went on so much, so she stuck with Bertha Stroud and Eleanor Ruck. Muriel said she had gone through that stage at fifteen, and expected Eunice would finish with them soon enough. But they read bits of each other's choices to each other and laughed about them.

For Eunice it was – she told Muriel, since it was only fair – the best time of her life. She knew it and always would. Perfect, but too perfect. The world was in turmoil, and she was having the time of her life because everything was in its place and organised down to the tiniest detail. A world ruined, and she had a job, and was with Muriel, both of them as snug as could be in their little box of a flat. There was something missing because it was so perfect.

'I wish you wouldn't go on using that word,' Muriel said. 'If I thought it was so perfect I would keep expecting something awful to happen.'

To be so content in a war, Eunice thought, seemed a sin. Not that that was it, either, admitting to herself that even if there hadn't been a war on she would have felt it was time to get out.

'I can't understand what you mean,' Muriel said.

'Well, I've tried to tell you.'

'I know, but I still don't think it's as easy a life as all that.'

The muted anguish in her tone suggested it was perhaps too perfect for her as well, but she didn't want to lose it by admitting it. She came out of the kitchen with two cups of Ovaltine. 'They're on war work at the factory, so we're doing our bit in the office to keep things going.'

'That's true.' Eunice was amazed, as if Muriel had listened in to her thoughts. She had seen an advert in the newspaper calling for women to join the ATS, and was going to apply, but didn't know how to tell Muriel. She would do it sooner or later, but decided to put it off for a time. 'I love it here with you, you know that.'

Muriel stirred her cup. 'And I like having you.'

Eunice knew, from the sharpness of her eyes, that Muriel could tell what was in the offing. Joining up – or not – was in everybody's mind, whether you were a man or a woman. She knew it would be strange, lonely, and most likely uncomfortable, but she wanted the adventure of a new life. If she had stayed in the lesser comfort at home she would have gone even sooner.

On Saturday afternoon they were walking along the bridleway towards Radcliffe, Muriel's favourite stroll which they had often done, talking about getting bikes and going long journeys around the countryside staying at youth hostels.

Humps of wet snow were held up by the bare twigs of the hedges, and they were well wrapped up in scarves and mittens. Eunice's words of decision were shaped in moisture as they came out of her full lips, irritated but almost crying herself at Muriel's tears.

HEADLINES VII

FRENCH GOVERNMENT MOVES TO VICHY.

17,000 GERMANS KILLED IN FRANCE.

1,900,000 FRENCH SOLDIERS TAKEN PRISONER.

GERMANS BOMB SOUTH WALES DOCKS.

HITLER'S FINAL APPEAL TO COMMON SENSE.

NAZI NEW ORDER FOR EUROPE.

DOVER BOMBED.

CIVILIAN CASUALTIES IN UK 258 KILLED
AND 321 INJURED.

THIRTEEN

'Bomb everybody dead!' Harry looked up, an openmouthed smile showing two teeth missing. 'Our Gillie's a tank.' A boost from thin arms sent the paper wing to the ceiling, and into a descending glide across the room.

'He thinks he's bombing the bleddy Germans,' Norma said. Trains were settling into and leaving the station at the bottom of the street, whiffs of locomotive smoke drifting in on the rattle of couplings. Gilbert stopped the next plane as if catching a ball aimed between goalposts, and wrung its neck. Disappointment blighted Harry's face, who had hoped his brother would join the game and send it just as skilfully back.

From two floors down came Leonard's arguing drone, then Sophie's accusing voice: 'You're jealous. You're bleddy jealous again.'

'Don't he go on?' Norma called from the bed. 'They've been like that for days.'

Harry tore another page from the atlas-gazetteer. 'He don't smack her in the chops like Dad used to.'

The floor was clean but the smell of dust was, Paul thought, the pong of damp wallpaper dried by a July sun from the open window. 'Me and our Ted would paste him if he did owt like that,' Norma said. 'Yo' would, as well, wouldn't you, our Gilbert?'

Paul found it hard to stay quiet, though he and his father between them would smack this lot down, or try. Like a serial on the pictures, if they were losing, Sam and Eunice would pile in – just in time.

Gilbert noticed the shade of a smile but said nothing, the peardrop smell of varnish with which Norma painted her nails reminding him that he was hungry. 'We had a slice of bread at breakfast time but there's been nowt since.'

'They forgot us.' Harry new-launched a plane that slid by Paul's

48

nose. Another tapped Gilbert on the eyebrow: 'Pack it in, or I'll smash yer.'

Harry sang: '*Rich bell, poor bell, bogeyman, thief,*' living in a world of his own.

'Where did you get those words?' Paul laughed.

'Don't know. Words don't cost owt.' Sophie said he knew no peril, and since a schoolmate had turned him onto making paper aeroplanes he did nothing else day in and day out, the atlas an inexhaustible wad of raw material. Three more were lined up on the runway. 'You'd think he was on war production,' Norma said.

Paul had sat reading the gazetteer on many an afternoon. 'Dad won't like you ripping it to pieces.'

'He'll have to lump it. He's too busy rowing with Mam. Just hark at him. They never stop.' His giggle echoed Norma, and he aimed another plane at the ceiling, chanting as he watched the flight: 'Doctor Leicester started to fester.'

Gilbert jumped up. 'I towd him to pack it in' – pushed him to the sill of the wide-open window, lifted him by both ankles and held him above the abyss of the backyard.

'Bring him in, and don't be so looney,' Norma shouted.

Paul rattled French coins in his pocket, but daren't call for him to be put down because Gilbert's arms trembled at the burden. The shock of a voice might cause him to let go, or he would drop him at the thought that he was being dared not to. Ordinary rules had nothing to do with someone like that.

Harry saw the brick wall of the house, and space below, and knew himself doomed if his brother opened the grip on his thin leg. Thinking he would be a goner any second he screamed his lungs to shreds, or so it seemed.

Leonard's upthrusting fist, puny from being so far down in the yard, and Norma's crack against Gilbert's ankle, made him pull Harry in, Gilbert's strength so much going that Paul had to help him to get Harry safe onto the floorboards.

The scene was long-lasting for Paul because Harry had gone limp after the first animal protests, and closed his eyes, though when Leonard came into the room the window was shut tight,

Norma back on the bed, Gilbert and Paul sitting on the floor, and Harry making the first fold of another aircraft.

Leonard stood in the doorway. 'If you do anything like that again in this house your feet won't touch the ground between here and borstal. That's about all the likes of you are bloody well fit for.'

'We was only having a bit o' fun,' Gilbert said.

He remembered worse pranks in the army. 'It's not much fun for Harry. You should have more sense, a lad of your age.'

Paul decided to get downstairs as soon as he could, not feeling the argument had much to do with him. 'He didn't drop him, did he?' Norma said.

They stuck together, at least. 'No, but he might have done, and then what would you say?'

'He'd be hanged for murder.' Harry's aeroplane flopped into Paul's lap, who unfolded it to read that there were too many lakes in Finland to be counted, and that people called Lapps lived in the northern part of the country with their reindeer.

As kids they had been dragged up, Leonard knew, and even with the best care in the world couldn't have turned out much different. A stint of the army might do them good, if the time ever came, though he couldn't see it doing much good for the army. If kids were so wicked to each other how could you expect them to alter and do any good at all when they grew up?

He walked downstairs with the remnant of his atlas-gazetteer, as if it were a wounded pet animal that might yet come back to life. He had spent five shillings on it when home from the war, to remind himself of all the nice places worth visiting in the world.

HEADLINES VIII

HITLER AND MUSSOLINI MEET AT THE BRENNER PASS.

GERMAN TROOPS ENTER ROUMANIA.

CHURCHILL SPEAKS.

GERMAN INVASION OF ENGLAND CALLED OFF.

CHURCHILL'S BROADCAST TO FRANCE.

HITLER MEETS FRANCO AT HENDAYE.

ITALY INVADES GREECE.

FOURTEEN

He had hoped for a quiet night, but the familiar wail warned workers and firewatchers alike, Moaning Minnie going at the same time as the guns. The Germans seemed able to find towns in the blackest of blackouts, but the ack-ack might as well send up grapeshot and canister for all they would hit.

Looking for fires from the top of the grain warehouse was like being on a cliff in front of an endless ocean. Your eyes were helped by noises you knew so well, except that with such a frost both ears were in danger of tinkling onto the railway lines a hundred feet below.

It was so bitter you almost hoped for a few incendiaries to warm you up, though even a funny idea like that got nowhere close to the cockles of your heart. He wore woollen combinations from throat to foot, a flannel shirt, waistcoat and cardigan; then a jacket, topcoat and tin hat, and boots over well-piled socks, but the scorching cold still got at your phizzog because you couldn't pad that up as well.

Even in daylight the January frost would blur your sight after fifty yards. Shunting trucks, the slide of wheels and the wheeze of engines, told him that stuff for war was moving, mail and bombs and food and tanks sorted and shifted – and a train twice as long as in peacetime not stopping at the station. The marshalling yards, Cammell Laird's gun factory, Boots' chemical works, Ericsson's wireless and telephone assembly, two big stations, and every kind of subcontracting engineering firm were set among acres of small and back-to-back houses, telling him that in an air raid anybody's number could be on a bomb.

Blades of light stabbed the big dark haystack of the sky, searching for planes inside. The glow-button of a shunting engine steamed out of a shed, and Leonard rubbed his eyes as if to clear all apprehension about Sophie and the kids.

Between the hollow pipe-like booming of lesser calibres, and shrapnel rattling onto steel rails and the roof around him, vibrations under his legs suggested that heavier stuff was coming down some way off, and twenty-odd years shrunk to flood his old-sweat tremors back. Sophie had asked him not to go on firewatching tonight, and he had replied that backsliding on Home Front duties could mean prison.

'Well,' she said, 'I wouldn't go if I didn't feel like it. And they wouldn't catch me, either.'

He laughed at the extent of her separation from the real world. If everybody was like that how could they win?

She stared as if he were betraying her. 'I sometimes wonder what bleddy difference it would make.'

'Well, there's a war on, anyway,' he said.

'You don't need to tell me.' Her bitter tone emphasised in no uncertain terms — and not only for him alone but for the wide world as well if it would listen — that her whole life had been a war, and that he was letting her down by not sharing her fight when it was more than his duty to do so.

She knew he was bound to be on nights or firewatching when the big raid came, and he couldn't say it wouldn't happen, because lots of other places had already had a pasting.

He let Albert Grindley do a stint, went back into the small room set apart from the vast floor piled high with sacks of grain. If you stood in the doorway you heard the scratch and scurry of rats, and now and again a squealing fight to the death as a savage but foolhardy cat cornered one of them.

Tom Bosely sat on a box with his head against the wall, a newly-married shunter who could hardly keep awake even when he was on the job in the sidings. The noise of the guns woke him. He felt in his pocket and slotted his dental plate back in, ran a hand through thick black hair and reached for his haversack. The partition rattled, so he ate the sandwich double-quick for fear they would get a direct hit and he would lose it during the trip to heaven.

Leonard looked at the spades, stirrup pumps and boxes of sand, and wondered how they would manage if thousands of tons of grain caught fire. They'd get roasted alive, so please God it wouldn't happen. 'It ain't a real raid,' he said. 'Hit and run by the sound of things.'

The guns grumbled, but there were no more bombs, the night not being fit for a dog to be out in. The council had reinforced the cellar at home with girders, and Sophie had watched him carry in fresh-cut planks, survivals of a repair job at his old allotment garden. Hammered together, they made a bench. And what cellar wasn't damp? He slapped on whitewash, and put down sacking, brought in a bag of candles and tacked blackout cloth made from canvas and blankets doubled at the grate. She pressed her hands to her side with laughing. 'Old soldiers never die!'

He hoped she was right, and on his way outside he met Mr Pearson the fire officer who asked him to go to Victoria Station and pick up a packet he needed from the post there. 'And put your tin hat on,' he said sharply – which cumbrous lid Leonard hated to wear, except when the danger was obvious. He took the chit from Pearson who, under his long black mackintosh, had on his usual pinstriped suit, collar and tie. He had a thin hard face, and never seemed to feel the cold. A look from his glinting eye and you either hit him so hard that you killed him, or did as you were told without grumbling. He was the sort of person every organisation needed, but Leonard had seen a sergeant like him shot in the back between the lines in France. The man who did it was killed by a shell a few seconds later, and only half the platoon got back. The alert was still on, and he didn't know why such thoughts came to him as he went through the streets.

Houses were as dark and silent as if abandoned. Fur awry and tail quivering straight, a cat walked from a doorway and sat in the middle of the street to clean its coat. Leonard, astonished at this homely action, put out his hand, grey-green eyes beamed to his soothing noises. He felt foolish, as if it would be shameful for anyone to see him.

The station was close to home so he would call in for a few minutes and make sure Sophie and the kids were all right. At shells bursting right overhead the cat sent out a paw as if Leonard caused its terror, tiny blades tearing his wrist. A man crossing the intersection with something under his coat walked more quickly on seeing Leonard with his helmet on. Rob all my comrades – how the thieves and blackmarketeers do get about. He remembered Pearson saying they should be shot. The cat leapt away too fast for him to give the kick it deserved.

Steadying the key, wrist throbbing from the cat's poisonous blow, it clicked and half turned. He had criss-crossed brown paper on all the windows and none had been broken so far during the alerts. For a bit of fun he went in shouting 'bring out your dead' knowing that only the living mattered. He kicked the cellar door to the wall, scraping along bricks till his jacket glowed from the whitewash. A plane drew another rattle of gunfire and he would say *there are worse things at sea*, but his lamp found the place empty.

Thanking God they had gone to the tougher concrete of a public shelter, he stood a moment to rouse himself from fatigue. Screening his lamp at the top of the stairs, he went into the room and found the bed a tangle of blankets but showing a movement at the ridge of mountains, then the whole range twitching as if water would burst from underneath.

Sophie moaned as he drew the clothes back, her kids like puppies in a basket. 'Shall we be killed, Mam?' chalk-faced Norma cried.

'It'll be better than being hanged.' Harry's small head showed above the rest. They nudged close at another earsplitting salvo. 'What a lot o' bangs there is, Leonard!'

O God our help in ages past – his laugh a disapproving mouth-open. 'You daft lot. It's only the guns, but there may be a raid later. You never know. So come on, and get out of it.'

Sophie put on her shoes, then came to him, the intense inner trembling heating her body. 'I'm ever so glad you've come back home, duck.'

At least they hadn't undressed, though he reached into a cupboard for a bundle of blankets because fear would make them colder in the cellar. His kiss was short. 'Don't be frightened. Just wait here.'

He ran to get Ivy and Paul. 'What are you two soft ninnies doing up here?'

'I don't care.' She was pale, and looked indignant, though he couldn't tell who at. He supposed it had to be God for putting her in danger, because it certainly couldn't be him for failing to provide safety from all of life's perils. He felt guilty nonetheless, and therefore angry. 'Let's have you down in the shelter.'

'I want to stay here.'

'You should look after your brother at least.' He pulled at her, though to put her in the damp cellar with her searing cough might be the worst option. 'Now come on.'

She didn't care. 'I know we won't get killed.'

'Well, I damned well don't. I've known plenty who thought that, and they aren't here any more.' The sleeping bundle of Paul was harder to rouse, and Leonard, who saw himself as not much older than him when he had gone off to war, yanked him eye-rubbing onto the floor and put shoes into his hands.

'There's a long long trail a-winding' – he sang like the Pied Piper till they were seated on planks as if waiting to have teeth pulled out at the dentist's. He cut bread and cheese and made the biggest pot of tea, down in one journey though burning his hand – for which he damned Pearson, who might think him a bit late when he got back.

'Can't you stay with us?'

Shrapnel swept slates and cobbles like a metal broom. He wanted nothing better than to press himself against her naked slack bosom and calm all her fears, their bodies burning into each other. 'You'll be safe enough here. There most likely won't be any bombs tonight.'

'I'm dying to pee,' Norma whimpered.

He had thought of everything. 'There's a pot under the bench.'

'If you piss yourself again' – Sophie looked around from her kiss with Leonard – 'you'll wash your own scruffy knickers.'

'I can't stay,' he told her. 'You know I've got to put in so many hours a week firewatching.'

'We won't get killed.' Harry held the candle to his face. 'I don't care about air raids, anyway. I'm going out to get some shrapnel soon. We can sell it a penny a lump at school.'

Gilbert nudged him. 'Shut-fucking-up!'

'You will get killed if you swear like that,' Leonard said.

'I suppose God's listening to me.' He pointed one finger upwards. 'Let Him, if He's got nowt better to do.'

They laughed, but Sophie's eyes softened with reproach. 'Just stay till the all-clear goes.'

He looked at them in the dim light of the candle, resolution melting in a choice nobody should have to make. 'I'll be in trouble if I don't get on with my errand. Maybe I shall in any case, if he thinks I'm overdue. But whether I go or stay, you'll be all right.'

Paul asked to go through the streets with him and see what the town looked like from the top of the grain warehouse – which would be better, he thought, than sitting like a rabbit in a hutch. He might be afraid if bombs began to fall, but even if they did they would miss him.

'You stay and help out here,' Leonard said.

He collected the packet, which smelled strongly of coffee, and followed his trail quickly back, thinking it was none of his business what was inside, marvelling at Sophie who had lacked the sense to get the kids to a safe place. Not that it would do any good to tell her off, though he would make them promise that next time the sirens went they'd get straight down to the cellar.

HEADLINES IX

ENEMY ATTACK TOBRUK.

LIVERPOOL BOMBED.

EVACUATION FROM GREECE.

RAF BOMB HAMBURG.

COLOGNE BOMBED.

BELFAST BOMBED.

HAILE SELASSIE ENTERS ADDIS ABABA.

MANNHEIM BOMBED.

VERY HEAVY RAID ON LONDON.

FIFTEEN

'It's marvellous,' Leonard said. 'Delicious. Even better than your corned beef stew last week.'

'I had to skin it, though. All that stuff coming out of its guts nearly made me sick. So if you find bits of fur in it, you'll know why.'

In Beryl's time he had often done the cooking, helped by Eunice, and not much cop had his part of the work been. 'It's the best stew I've tasted.'

'I was walking up Wilford Road and saw this bloke outside a pub selling them for a couple of bob each. So I bought one. It saves on the rations.'

Norma cleaned her spoon with a piece of bread. 'I'll bet it's somebody's tabby cat.'

'I don't care,' Gilbert said. 'It still tastes nice.'

A macaroni pudding with currants and raisins followed. 'You'll fatten me up,' Leonard said.

She leaned over for a kiss. 'You could do with it, duck. The more there is of you the better I like it.'

'I think we'll have to wait to get me any fatter until the war's over.' He noted the familiar, sly kind of tenderness in her smile, which he didn't altogether trust, yet could not exist without. Reminded of how she often turned it on any stranger who spoke to her in the club, it was nevertheless her one way of showing intimate concern, and he couldn't help but feel that only he had the right to it.

She could barely credit the fact that there were books in the house: a Bible, various hymnals, and a remnant of the atlas-gazetteer. When Paul was looking at a map she took the handbook on shunting off the shelf and said: 'Open this one, and see how hard it is.'

He already knew, because his father read it assiduously now and again to try for promotion at work. Wanting to please her, he flipped through the complex diagrams, each paragraph of writing numbered. 'I don't understand it, though.'

'Ah, but your father does!'

Leonard was softened by her simple faith in print. 'It's not difficult when you've been in the job as long as I have.'

She put the book gently down, and with her hand still on it said: 'I got a ten-shilling postal order from Charlie this morning. I couldn't believe it at first, but I suppose his conscience must have been pricking him about the kids. I think I'd rather manage without his money, though.'

'We could do with it sometimes.' Ivy wanted to make life easier, knowing they were settled with Sophie and her kids and that nobody could do anything about it. She had seen her father and Sophie going down the street holding hands. Another time Sophie walked with both hands on his arms, a pose so unnatural that Ivy was glad that they turned the corner.

Sophie sat down to her portion of food. 'I expect you're right. They're his bleddy kids, after all. He gets away with murder – like all men. It isn't right.'

Leonard could not dispute her sense of justice. 'Did he send a letter?'

'Only a bit of paper with his name on it.'

'No address?'

'I know the pubs he haunts. Not that I'll ever want to find him. He's a real bad 'un, he is, and always has been. You're worth a hundred of him, duck.'

He was glad to hear it, though the more she said so the more difficult he found it to believe, he didn't know why. Sometimes he could hardly fathom why he was in the world, asking the question, when he did, with his whole being. He undid his waistcoat. 'Still, he sent you ten bob. I suppose we must give him credit for something. Do you want me to go and cash it at the post office?'

'I did that as soon as I got it.' She spoke with annoyance, as if she'd had enough of the topic, and he wondered why this should be, till he remembered her not liking to talk very long about anything.

They managed better these days, five children between them

or not, because Sophie worked as an assistant cook at a British Restaurant, earning nearly three pounds a week, as well as bringing home the odd bag of flour or sugar, tea or minced meat which she pinned under her skirt. 'They find a bit over every so often, and divide it up between us. I'm glad of it, to tell you the truth. I get fed up queuing for every bit of this or that.'

Sugar in his tea more times than the ration could have allowed, he only hoped she wouldn't get caught, because if there was any surplus these days it surely wouldn't get distributed down to the level she worked on.

HEADLINES X

RUDOLF HESS FLIES TO SCOTLAND.

VERY HEAVY RAID ON LONDON.

GERMAN AIRCRAFT REPORTED IN IRAQ.

HANOVER BOMBED.

GERMANS INVADE CRETE.

HMS *HOOD* BLOWN UP.

BISMARCK SUNK.

UR OCCUPIED BY BRITISH TROOPS.

IRAQI REVOLT COLLAPSES.

SIXTEEN

The lame-dog engine note signified more than a couple circling for the kill. Long hours remained before daylight, calm outside but terror within being the tale of his life. He had learned to keep both states apart, though the hellish noise could never become normal, nerves in your skin and bones, and no real fear, unless fear was that pit in your stomach as big as the universe. But these nights the guns were never silent – otherwise why would they be made? – and always going pot-and-kettle somewhere.

A whistle so loud he wanted to reach and turn the oscillating wireless off: but it was halfway down and joined by another demon eager for the chorus, such an expanding screech that, unable to tell the direction, he ran like the Artful Dodger to evade the blast.

The bombs were further off than he had supposed, beyond the station maybe – so what are you doing pressed against creosoted sleepers under a flatcar because it came closer than you liked?

A flower of smoke danced above the approaching pilot-engine (under the long bridge the station going beams and cinders to the clouds) but he went on with reckoning the debit and credit of goods for war, booting down all worry for Sophie and the kids who might already be too crushed by rubble to cry. Pig-ignorant, snotty and dead cheeky much of the time they were, but right now he loved them all, craved to run between gunfire and falling buildings to make sure they were still alive, though could he put out both hands to catch the falling bombs and throw them back? A horse-like piss by a track rarely caught him midshift, but he hurried the buttoning-up.

He would have twigged the gait anywhere, though the greeting was split by thunderclapping salvoes bursting across the river. 'Did you think I was hiding from the old bang-bangs up there?'

'Well, we used to in France when we could, didn't we?' Albert

Grindley put a hand on his shoulder. 'It's a right bleddy packet. Makes you feel like putting a wet sack over your noddle.'

'At least we can see better with their flares.' Nice to have 'em now and again. Not to mention the flames from Boots' factory which coloured the sky orange and green. 'How is it at the sheds?' Leonard yelled at his ear, the flesh tickling his lips.

'Murder. I'm off there now, to shunt some trucks in. Old Arthur White must be up to his neck in it.'

'I expect he is.' The job was so hard that shunters were at a premium, and some like Tom Bosely, being young and strong, had been let off military service. The shunting trucks twisted in the storm, jaggling their protest. He licked paper lips, and turned from another close blast to finish his chalkings, the shunters' locomotive bleating a melancholy lost sheep note near the station, where they would be rolling stock into the clear before the whole lot went up like Hill-bloody-Sixty and no mistake.

The squat Castle, illuminated on its high rock by various fires, would never come to harm, though God alone could say how strong the mortar was between the bricks in his own house, powdery sand at the scrape of a fingernail, and ceiling all of a tremble when a lorry went by. Girders wouldn't hold under the weight: hair slicked by blood, cap torn, wireless valves scattered, cups smashed, tablecloth sagging with plaster, bones tearing through: a dream-vision momentarily packed before the eyes. Every bomb got some family, but the best thing was to be so busy that you forgot to worry, or even to tick yourself off when you felt like running.

A whistle announced the advent of impending doom, growling planes not going till no brick stood on another. The whistle grew to a scream as if someone tied to a line heard the Silver Jubilee that no pointsman could switch into the clear. He got under a wagon but the noise stopped clean, as if the bomb had changed its mind and gone back up. A dud – and a good half mile away at that. Probably hit the mud somewhere.

Albert Grindley's shadow went with can and rag between the wheels, while those in the sheds tapped and bodged in light never light enough yet too light under a rosette of flame from houses across the canal: fire engines and an ambulance on the bridge screeching around the rubble and glass, police whistles puny but urgent.

The bugs, rats and blackclocks must be all of a scramble in such old back-to-backs that were hit. Even if he went home he wouldn't be able to stay, and they could be killed after he got back. Leave the firestep of a trench and you'd be shot for it. And fair enough, because you let your pals down. A pinlight from Albert's unnecessary lamp: 'You jammy bogger, it's a bit quieter round here. Me and Tom had a close call on the other side.'

'We did,' Tom said. 'I'm worried about my missis. She's just had a young 'un. Got any fags on you?'

Impossible a plane could exist with so many chasing shells, the racket nearly as deafening as one of the old barrages. Poor Beryl had missed all this, and who could feel fear at it when she had gone before him? Wherever she was, if she was anywhere (and where that was he didn't honestly think he would ever know) she was safer than him, and though he should be glad, there was still much of him that wasn't. He could save his own cigarette till later. 'Keep it covered, though.'

'You don't need to tell me,' he said ungratefully, hand shaking as he lit up by a wheel. 'I live only a couple of streets away, so anybody mind if I nip to see if everything's all right? I shan't be more than a couple o' minutes.'

You couldn't hear the planes, as if the Royal Artillery had found fifty more guns to open up from behind Jacky Pownall's scrapyard. 'Worried, are you?' said Albert, giving Leonard a wink.

'About them I am.'

'He won't be missed,' Leonard said.

'And if they do get you on the carpet, I'll put in as good a word as I can before they stand you up against a wall at dawn and pop you off.'

'I knew I could rely on you two,' and he ran towards the gate before they could say another word.

Half a dozen trucks were caught by a shower of incendiaries, and they worked to shunt them away from an ammunition train a few tracks parallel. After the all-clear the inspector gave them a nod of thanks, which Tom Bosely had got back in time to receive, Leonard was glad to note.

HEADLINES XI

RAF BOMB BERLIN.

EDEN WARNS JAPAN.

GERMAN TROOPS FORTY MILES FROM THE BLACK SEA.

ATLANTIC CHARTER.

CHURCHILL'S MESSAGE OF SUPPORT TO STALIN.

ATTACK ON LENINGRAD BEGINS.

BRITISH AND RUSSIAN TROOPS ENTER IRAN.

RUSSIANS EVACUATE NOVGOROD.

BRITISH GOVERNMENT TAKE OVER ALL RAILWAYS FOR THE DURATION.

SEVENTEEN

Why do they always come at mealtimes? Leonard wondered. Sophie's eldest, called Ted, was of medium height and well built, with fair hair and observant white-blue eyes.

'What do *you* want?' Sophie asked.

'I've come to see how you are, Mam.'

'You've seen me. Now you can go.'

Her tone was such that Leonard asked himself whether Ted hadn't done something unforgivable against her before she came to live with him, though he knew it wasn't the moment to make enquiries.

'Dad chucked me out,' Ted responded, 'so that he could be alone with his new fancy woman. He thought I might have a go at her myself. Not that I'd mind. She's a lovely bit of stuff. Works at the gun factory.'

'You can piss off' – such venom causing her lips to tremble – 'we don't want you starting trouble here.'

The notion that he was thought capable of it seemed to excite him. 'Dad said *he* might call one of these days to see how you are.'

Ash fell from her cigarette. 'Let the swine try, and see where it gets him. I don't give a sod, though, for him or anybody.'

Leonard felt this to be a wonder, that she would say such a thing, and mean it so vehemently. She was the kind of free spirit he'd had no experience of before, a state of mind, especially in a woman, that fascinated him. Yet two questions occurred: was she really never able to give a damn for anybody? And if she was would she one day say it so as to include him? He decided that the answer to the first question must be no, in which case he would never have anything to fear from his uncertainty about the second.

Ted's lively eyes focused on the stewpot and loaf, then at Ivy who wouldn't meet his gaze. 'I ain't got nowhere to go, and it's chucking it down outside.'

'You could find lodgings,' Leonard suggested.

Ted stared, as if noticing him for the first time, and not much liking what he saw. 'It ain't easy these days. Anyway, I'm skint.'

Sophie had mentioned that he worked on building sites driving a dumper truck. 'You can pay when you get your wages,' Leonard said. 'They let you do that these days, if you look decent enough,' which he did, in sports coat and flannels, though he wore no tie.

Ted ignored him. 'That stew smells lovely, Mam.'

She went into the scullery for a plate and spoon. 'You can have some. Then out you bleddy-well go.'

He tapped Harry, to indicate he wanted a chair.

'Leave me alone.'

Norma slid from hers. 'Sit here, our Ted.'

His nose close to the steaming food: 'I knew you wouldn't turn me away without a crust, Mam!'

'Don't think you're staying' – though her voice was less harsh as she cleared pots from the table. 'We can't put you up here. There ain't room.'

The issue was taken too easily from Leonard's control, because not only could he not tell someone they couldn't stay in the house, but he couldn't even inform them that they could. He knew, however, from Sophie's generous feeding of her son, that she would wangle him into board and lodging before the evening was much older, and said: 'He can have the top back room for a night or two. It's empty except for a chair and that truckle bed. I'm sure he can manage.'

Neither a nod nor a thank you came from either, confirming to Leonard that they were a strange lot. He was only doing it to please Sophie, and hoped they weren't going to quarrel simply because he was arguing in favour of something she already wanted. Being deprived of making the fight herself to get Ted into shelter, in order to prove the love she should have for him, it was nevertheless obvious that she disliked him. Leonard decided they could sort the matter out between them, which he thought them well able to do.

'There aren't any blankets,' she said.

Ted raised his head from the dish, fork prongs upright as if ready-aye-ready should the Devil come down to make an attempt on him. 'Go out and buy me some, then. The pawnshop's still open.'

'Buy 'em yourself,' she said, 'out of your wages.'

'He'll thieve some.' Gilbert spoke as if he too had a grievance against him, though Leonard supposed it to be their normal form of conversation.

'Shurrup, you snipe-nosed jumped-up fuckpig, or I'll throttle you.'

'He can take a couple from the air raid shelter,' Leonard suggested.

Ted folded a piece of sliced bread and wiped his plate clean. 'Got any fags, Mam?'

'Buy your own, you mingy bleeder – if you can find any in the shops.'

'Funny,' he grinned, 'I thought you'd say summat like that.'

'What have you done with all your money?'

'Lost it in the bookies. Spent it on tarts in the boozer. It's gone up in smoke.' He laughed. 'What did you think? I might be dead next week.'

He meant trouble, and she wasn't happy that Leonard had mentioned the top back room. Charlie and the kids had always made her life a misery, though there had never seemed anything she could do about it. Leonard sensed her mood, but couldn't unsay his words. He only had one cigarette, and that was for his break during the shift.

At some unspecified time of the long dark night the wish for a smoke set him crouching by a flatcar, but for something more than a smoke, for he would hold the cigarette between his hands, his breath drawing the tip into an orange lantern, seeing between the fingers a world glowing like his soul in the prison of the blackout, the soul warm and free in the world which imprisoned it.

HEADLINES XII

TUC PLEDGE THAT THE WORKERS
WILL FIGHT TO THE END.

AIR RAIDS ON MALTA.

CHURCHILL'S REVIEW OF THE WAR.

FIRST SNOWFALL ON RUSSIAN FRONT.

AIR RAID ON CAIRO.

GERMANS OCCUPY KIEV.

FORMER MOSLEM MUFTI OF JERUSALEM
TAKES REFUGE FROM BRITISH POLICE
IN THE JAPANESE LEGATION.

EIGHTEEN

He felt like a human being when he was on days, getting up at six and making breakfast for himself, and for Ted who had stayed on because, as he said to Sophie, I like your cooking. With his two pounds a week board, plus Leonard's wages, as well as the few pounds Sophie brought in, and the occasional postal order she told him that Charlie had sent, they had enough money, because nowadays there wasn't all that much to spend it on.

Leonard took off his cap and coat one evening to find nothing cooked either for him or the rest of them. 'Any idea where Sophie is?'

'I expect she's leaning on the bar of The Eight Bells, and having a good laugh.' Ted stretched himself in the armchair. 'Or some place like that.'

Ivy was preparing cabbage and potatoes, realising at last that somebody would have to do it. 'She went out.'

'Did she say why?'

'Not to me.'

'I told you' — and Ted seemed delighted to do so — 'she's gone to the boozer.'

'What for?' He hardly knew why he bothered to ask.

Ted laughed so long that Leonard felt a dangerous urge to strike him. 'If you don't know, I don't.'

'She said she would be back before you got home.' Ivy wanted an explosion that would scatter them far away, but shook inwardly with fear at the prospect of violence. She laid cold white sausages in the pan with a piece of lard, took a match from the eggcup on the shelf and struck it along the stove top, the circle of holes sprouting blue fire. 'She wanted to get summat from the shop, I suppose.'

'Why didn't you say so at first?' He poured a cup of tea, but half an hour later knew that all shops had long since been closed. After supper, and the nine o'clock news, he put on his coat.

He had heard The Eight Bells referred to as the town's premier knocking shop, and thought it might well be so as he stood in the smoky public bar making a bad job of trying to see through the crowd, noting that some soldiers wore the better cloth of Australians. About to leave, he heard Sophie's unmistakable come-one-and-come-all laugh which had sounded so attractive when meant for him alone.

Ease of mind in such a place was impossible, certainly not on one's own. He wasn't afraid of any individual, but felt little tolerance of the unpredictable shift of a crowd's mood, the sort of laughter that any second could brew into a fight. He made his way through the room, knowing she was in it somewhere.

A roll of dark hair showed from under her headscarf, and she was made up with rouge and powder, lipstick outlining her fullish mouth, a white blouse fastened by a brooch. Two smart young sergeants, one Australian and the other English, stood close. She laughed again, and took a swig of her gin-and-It. 'I love you both.'

'But you've got to make up your mind, darling. It's got to be him, or me.'

The Englishman was as cocky as all get-out. 'I thought she'd done it already, pal.'

She saw this chap, who was certainly no stranger, giving her a very queer look, a man with a face as long as a fiddle, and a greying quiff of hair, wearing dark work trousers and waistcoat, and a railwayman's jacket, who didn't seem to know whether he should break her neck or go away and forget her. She didn't want him to do either, but her smile turned into a hardness of mouth he hadn't seen before. Such a shape was more than matched, however, by his own. 'Are you coming, or aren't you?'

The sergeants signalled a wink and lift of the shoulders, to agree that something might not be all right. Perhaps they were early on in their pints, Leonard thought, or couldn't switch, soldiers or not, from gay blades to raging belligerents. Sensing an unstoppable anger in Leonard once it got going, they looked away as if the issue didn't concern them.

She finished her drink and touched both their arms. 'He's the one I choose. It's my husband. Have a nice time, lads. Abyssinia!'

He didn't care whether she followed or not, yet knew she would. It wasn't the first time she had gone drinking while he was out, and undoubtedly got up to something. Whatever he did – and it was beyond him, he thought with a self-satisfaction he couldn't altogether take to, ever to hit a woman – she would most likely do it again, because he couldn't be in the house all the time.

In the street he swung with fist lifted, but to frighten, he told himself, to threaten, trapezing thoughts cursing him for a bully and a fool when she cringed as if he could do no other than half-kill her.

'I came out for a drink,' she said, 'that's all' – reading his change of mind. 'There's nothing wrong with that, is there? I get so fed up sitting in every night. I want a bit o' company now and again.'

It was hard to breathe, control what he would. 'Next time you feel that way, tell me, and I can come with you. It's not respectable for a woman to be on her own in a pub these days, and you know it.' The intended sermon gave way to her laugh, this time so meant for him alone that he could not stop his own laughter. She squeezed his arm, agreeing with all he said. Most of the time she couldn't make him out because he looked anything between a contented clown and a tragic idiot. 'I love you,' she told him. 'You're the only one I love.'

Since he lived but to hear her say it he must love her as well, walking home with a mutual warmth that shut out any hatred. She was, after all, living with him, and no man could complain about that.

HEADLINES XIII

GERMANS ASSAULT CRIMEA AT DAWN.

4,000 ITALIANS CAPTURED IN ABYSSINIA.

WAVELL AND AUCHINLECK CONFER IN BAGHDAD.

MARTIAL LAW IN PRAGUE.

BRITISH ASSOCIATION ADOPTS CHARTER OF
SCIENTIFIC PRINCIPLES.

RAF BOMB STETTIN.

REPORT ON EMPIRE AIR TRAINING SCHEME.

UK CIVILIAN CASUALTIES IN SEPTEMBER 217 KILLED
269 INJURED.

RAF BOMB STUTTGART.

NINETEEN

She was a long time gone to pee so he got up to find out why. Even if it was to change her sanitary towel she should be back by now. If he met her in the yard he would say he was off to the same place, in case she guessed he was checking her whereabouts. What she called his blind jealousy (although he rarely felt the need of a white stick and a dog to follow it up) had caused such ructions lately that he would be as unseen as if in no-man's-land.

It was so dark that the shadowy grain of movement baffled him at first, but someone was pressing her against the wall, her arms full around him. A pang of torment at their obliviousness of him so near brought out his cry. 'What the hell's all this?'

The man slid under him, giving a push that met air, and was through the gate hoping to vanish like the snake he was. But Leonard shot a boot forward, causing him to fall. Leonard pushed. Leonard sat on him, giving something to remember left and right against his head, till in one wider swing he glimpsed Sophie – the moon uncurtained by a cloud – looking from the gate, pale and bitter at his violence, scared as if she had seen too much and knew it could never be stopped, a vision of searing hopelessness.

The man crying to be left alone was younger than them both, and Leonard, being sure she had brought it on, sprang away in one movement and let him go.

Charlie in the old days would hit her on catching her, a black eye more than once, but had never tackled the man. 'You call that talking to him?' Leonard bawled as they walked out of the gate, glad of the moon's convenient vanishing so that nobody could see who was making such a row. 'And God knows what else. I'm not blind. Nor deaf, either.'

Her heart was full, a single tear of passion clinging to her cheek. He would never understand. The man had been an old flame, her previous feelings rushing back. Leonard hadn't seen the flicker of their eyes in the saloon, one head nodding towards the door, and then the other, oh so sly and full of meaning. She had kissed him without being sure he wanted her to, hoped Leonard hadn't hurt him too much for something the poor chap hadn't even had. 'I was only saying goodnight.'

He hung his coat behind the scullery door. A few more moments and he would have caught them at something worse. Then he might have killed them both, his heart drumming at the thought. 'It's not damned well right, and you ought to know it.'

Ted got up from Leonard's armchair, his voice alien enough to separate them. 'What ain't right, Mam?'

'Nothing,' she said, 'as far as you're concerned.'

Ivy was glad to see her father, because Ted had been trying to kiss her all evening. She sat reading *The Oracle*, bent forward with a hand over her knees. Ted turned to her because she still seemed too far out of the world to take proper notice of him, and that couldn't be right. 'Rustle us up some bread and cheese, duck. A bucket o' tea as well, while you're at it.' His eyes appeared closer together than usual, a small triangle with upturned nose over the hard lines of his mouth as he leaned against the mantelpiece. 'It's like a grave in here.'

'You know what you can do if you don't like it.' Leonard went on to suggest that there must be plenty of cheerful lodging places in town.

The house was as tight as a prison to Sophie: Leonard's furniture among which she sat, Leonard's mirror in which she saw herself more and more as the tethered victim unable to do as she liked which was the only way she knew of making his life easy; and Leonard's bed in which, because of his intolerance, she felt a stranger no matter how nice she was to him. 'Every time I go out he gets on at me. I can't even look at another bloke, never mind speak to one.'

'Is that what you call it?' His hand shook as he lit a cigarette.

'You're too jealous to live with.'

'There's a need to be, as well.'

Ted, facing the mirror, lifted his hands as if to conduct the Hallé Orchestra, then sang *Jealousy* in his best party voice, till Ivy told him to pack it in. 'I wondered when I was going to get a dicky-bird out of you,' he said, and only stopped singing when Sophie put the teapot on the table and began to laugh – otherwise she would cry, and what was the good of that?

Leonard knew he must endure such mockery, whatever shame his children saw him suffer, but could not hold back from saying: 'It might be a good idea if you packed up your stuff and cleared off. You're no longer welcome in this house.'

Let him live in the street and see how he liked it, if he couldn't behave himself. He felt pitiless towards him, though knew he ought not to. Looking into his room he had seen the bed littered with French letter packets and copies of *Health and Efficiency*. A pair of overalls and workshirts were stuffed in a corner, one good suit draped over a chairback. He earned more than enough to support himself in lodgings, and a couple of carrier bags would suffice for him to move his stuff.

'If he goes,' Sophie said, 'I go.'

So that was it. The words were there, but he couldn't say them: *Go, then. Take your unruly kids with you, and leave me in peace.* Ivy willed him to speak, hands by her side to let the thought fly more easily from her heart. But he didn't, wouldn't, could not, features fixed so as not to reflect the inner fire which needed more than a bucket of sand and a stirrup pump to douse it out.

Sophie fell for any personable man who said a half-kind word, or she pretended to, didn't know the difference, anybody was her meat, and it was either stay or go, because there was nothing else he could do about it, even though he felt Ivy, with tears at her eyes, willing him to sling them out.

'I'm sure he would be happier living somewhere else.' He couldn't believe his voice, yet must, since everyone else detected the wreckage of his pride.

'You'd better be careful how you behave,' Sophie said to her son, 'and stop tormenting people. If you don't, I'll be the one to chuck you and your rubbish into the street, and then you'll bleddy-well have to go.'

It was hardly peace at any price, but for the moment it would have to do, Leonard consoling himself with the thought that no matter how badly she carried on she was still the queen of the house.

HEADLINES XIV

HITLER'S ORDER OF THE DAY TO TROOPS FACING
MOSCOW: TODAY IS THE BEGINNING OF THE LAST
GREAT DECISIVE BATTLE OF THIS YEAR.

GERMAN ATROCITIES IN CRETE.

SOVIET GOVERNMENT LEAVES MOSCOW.

FIFTY HOSTAGES SHOT IN NANTES.

RAF BOMB HAMBURG.

GERMANS CAPTURE KHARKOV.

TWENTY

The chapel on Gell Street had been turned into a British Restaurant for a war that seemed to be going on forever, though so far it was only half as long as the last one. He had been a few times with Beryl and the kids in the old days to hear the marvellous preaching of Arthur Scorton, a treat for the ears and the heart as scriptural denunciations of the mad dog world came out of Scorton's golden mouth wrapped in precepts that made you want to live rather than throw yourself off Trent Bridge or Castle Rock. Religion hadn't been particularly it, but the pure and active language made you think, and calmed the week before the next Sabbath came.

But these days he thought only of Sophie, occasionally stopped work to wonder where in what part of the world he was, and how to cross that canyon of time and space to get back into the work at hand.

He joined youths, women and elderly men from various factories converging on the same chapel to get something into their bellies. When on nights he knew she went out, but there was nothing he could do, because she told him often enough that she wasn't a dog to be tethered to his will. On the other hand he told her that neither was he a dog to be chained to her whims. Words in his mind were more reasonable than those bellowed in frequent rows. Nor could he pull himself back from the forward march of his feet, though knowing it would be best. With Sophie he had to form every sentence clearly before he spoke, and decide whether or not to let it go, which he couldn't recall having done in the past, though in those days – wondering if any had in fact existed – he hadn't had such confrontations to harrow him, because he and Beryl lived with similar ideas. Jealousy was new, and the pitch of his rage frightened him so much that he was able to calm himself.

At work he put in what overtime he could, and these days there was plenty, or he did as little as possible in order to know what

Sophie was up to. She preferred him being locked into overtime, or on nights, or firewatching, a system which meant more money for the house, since less was spent on drink when he felt obliged to take her out. The anxiety in any case varied, for what cause he did not know. Lack of a pattern in her moods sometimes drove him close to madness. Or he couldn't care what she did, which disturbed him even more.

She earned her own money and put in so lavishly for the housekeeping, as well as paying for an occasional foray to the pub, that he wondered whether she didn't earn far more than he did, and if so where it came from.

Such reasoning stopped him, as if pole-axed, rain splashing from his cape, certain assumptions going like a clutch of poisoned spears in his side. He walked on, work to be done, useless to worry about what you could not control, wondering whether such crippling notions had only maddened him because of a full moon, or claptrap rubbish like that.

The queue moved, women in white aprons and caps setting out shilling meals, smells making him hungry after a morning's work. He expected Sophie to be one of the servers, though not wanting to be seen in case she assumed he was on the prowl to check where she was.

Going forward, he had a right to do as he liked, and to spend more time at the counter he took soup, and a plate of mash, mincemeat and carrots. 'Is there someone called Sophie who works here?'

A short thin woman, whose face looked as if she had walked fifty miles through a frosty wind, a roll of swarf-grey hair showing under her white snood, seemed not to have heard above the clatter. 'Sophie Waterall,' he leaned closer, 'she works here. Where is she?'

Deciding he wasn't barmy and that there was no need to get the police, she called along the line: 'Anybody heard of Sophie Waterall?'

Perhaps she had used another name. 'She was tall, with dark hair, and well built.'

'Come on, mate, get a move on. There's a war to be won.'

Leonard turned, to fix a stare at a man who was certainly not above military age. 'Well, go and win it, then.' At the till he took a quarter-piece of bread for his soup. 'You must know her.'

She ladled out spotted dick and custard. 'Oh, I twig who you mean now. Do you remember her, Betty?'

Betty was a pretty young girl with long auburn hair, but her laugh was harsh. 'It was months ago. She only worked here for a week. She got the push for being too light fingered. Got greedy, I suppose. She was a good laugh, though. Yeh, I remember her right enough.'

Thinking why hadn't they said so sooner, he ate a meal for the toothless, nothing on his mind but Sophie, knifing and forking as little use as the walk back to work in telling him what was the matter, so he got on his feet because others wanted his place at the oilcloth.

He cut into the familiar smell of locomotive smoke in Middle Furlong Road, knowing there was only one way to get the money she had lately been so flush with, a method mortifying to him who lived with her. He tried to understand what made her the way she was, but the reasons were as numerous as cobblestones on the road, because for which one could he throw her into the street and tell her to destroy somebody else? You had to go through the mill to know what made someone do the things they did. But what if she would never reveal the reason for it? Or what if he was never able to find out why? Or what if there was nothing special that made her tick? Or what if even she would never be able to say what made her tick, even though she might want to, and even though he put up with her for twenty more years? She was like everyone else, even like him, in that she lived not knowing or caring what effect she had on others.

She was just herself, as he had always known, but he would be in torment forever if he couldn't discover why that was, though hoping to would be the only proof that he loved her. He passed between the gateposts into the goods yard, horrified at the way she carried on, not being a fool, or a stone, because even if you knew what made someone tick, and they themselves knew what it was, and you yourself knew absolutely what made you the way you were, things would go on just the same.

Maybe it would be easier if he abandoned the house and looked back on the experience as the no-man's-land of his life, thanking God he was as free of torment as Europe would be when they got it back from the Germans. But he didn't want to go as a way of getting his own back, would only pack up and get out if he had something better to look forward to. The trouble was he only knew what he wanted to do when he was happy, in which case he was content the way things were and didn't want to do anything.

HEADLINES XV

MERSEYSIDE BOMBED.

US LOANS USSR ONE THOUSAND MILLION DOLLARS.

HMS *ARK ROYAL* SUNK OFF GIBRALTAR.

EIGHTH ARMY ADVANCES IN LIBYA.

TWENTY-THREE THOUSAND ITALIANS SURRENDER
AT GONDAR.

MALTA HAS ITS THOUSANDTH ALERT.

TWENTY-ONE

Keeping the tracks in order was a job that never stopped. He had been doing it for a long time and so was efficient. The tracks in his mind he knew also, though couldn't sort them out half as well. Rolling stock was set aside to let troop trains through: loads of equipment, flatcars of tanks, fuel wagons and trucks of coal were listed and sorted and sent on their way. Normal services continued as far as possible because soldiers moved to and from their leave. By the end of the day he was famished and exhausted, lucky to get the last bus home at nine, though he walked upright into the house.

Ivy stood away from the table to give him space, gentle with him after his day. 'Your dinner's nearly cold, Dad. I'll warm it up for a bit.'

He hung his haversack behind the door and balanced his cap on the rolled arm of the sofa. A letter once a month from Sam in the Marines let them know that he was, thank God, all right. He sat to read the small page that was more than welcome but which gave little idea as to where in the world he was, but Leonard always hoped to come in from work one day and see him sitting at the table with his tunic open, hair combed smartly down, face full and healthy, rifle and kit propped in a corner. The picture troubled him only in so far as he wondered how Sam would take to Sophie and her kids. Ted would have to go, for a start, to provide him with a bed.

But the sight of Sam would help Ivy, maybe even cure her more ominous cough. She hunched by the fire, hand to her mouth, and cheeks pink through the white skin, returning the handkerchief to her pinafore pocket without caring to look. He heard her at night, unable to sleep. The doctor had stood her off work, and sent her with a letter to the outpatients department for an X-ray. She had similar features to her mother, which made him happy and unhappy at the same time, because while he was glad to be reminded of better days, he could see her going into a state he hardly dared think about. Trying not to dwell on earlier times made it easy to hold such happiness at a distance.

He looked around. 'Where's Paul?'

'It's his Scouts' night.'

'He's learning how to make a fire out of two sticks, I expect.' Norma lay on the couch paring her nails. 'We ought to buy him a box o' matches for his birthday.'

'At least he's learning something.' She didn't even know when Paul's birthday was. 'And Sophie, where is she?'

Ivy thought she might be doing overtime at the restaurant. She often did.

'She hasn't been near the place in months.' Energy came back with his meal of spuds and parsnips, and meat which gravy hardly moistened. Ivy did her best with what was in the shops, and in any case you didn't complain as long as it was good enough to put into your mouth. It would have been even better if there was food of the spiritual kind which gave peace of mind. When you cared for someone and couldn't live without her, and looked after your children, and trusted that they felt the same towards you, then that should be repletion indeed. In the old days he went to chapel now and again with Beryl, and took the children so that they should grow up thanking God they were well shod and fed, since who else could they be grateful to when parents tried so hard?

The emptiness of the house without Sophie took away his reason for being alive. After the others were in bed, the crying of a baby next door increased his desolation, so he read in the newspaper of how the Red Army was smashing the Germans in the snow near Moscow, which couldn't be anything but good if it got the war over soon. He also read that a man had got two years in jail for robbery. If he had known the true nature of the world would he have chosen to be born into it? There was no option, and the world was what people made it. You did what you could and hoped others would put in their bit as well, but too many did otherwise, not realising the evil they caused, incapable of doing anything about it even so. He rehearsed phrases to attack her with, but when she came in his measured words would turn wild with wrath.

Cold ash fell into the pan under the grate, but it was too late to restock the fire, and little coal was left till the ration dropped into the cellar on Friday. In the encroaching chill endless self-talk did not displease him because such time passed could not return to torment him again. On first hearing her laugh and seeing her face he fell for her because he thought anyone with such humour could not be immoral. Impossible to know that she found it as easy to lie as to tell the truth, but he supposed she needed something stronger than either so as to know she was really living.

He was too tired to go and look for her, feared open space more than protecting walls. Maybe she was waiting for him to search, as proof that he loved her enough to risk her mockery. She could laugh that he had chased her around the streets because he was jealous. He no longer cared, not to the extent of amusing everybody when he dragged her out of a pub by her hair, and he would be glad if she left him because he wasn't willing to provide such excitement.

A clock set daily by the six pips, between its scrolls of marble casing on the shelf, was a wedding present from Beryl's family. Sophie wouldn't care how many objects reminded him of a different set of people. It was a minute to midnight, and further rehearsals of what he would say were useless. He ran a poker through the ash to be sure it was dead and, having to make the usual early start, took off his boots and went upstairs.

HEADLINES XVI

UNITED NATIONS DECLARATION.

JAPANESE LAND ON WEST COAST OF MALAYA.

MOLOTOV GIVES DETAILS OF GERMAN ATROCITIES
IN RUSSIA.

RAF REGIMENT FORMED.

AUSTRALIA DECLARES WAR ON BULGARIA.

HITLER HAS ONLY GOT ONE BALL – OFFICIAL.

US ARMY TO BE RAISED TO THREE MILLION SIX
HUNDRED THOUSAND MEN.

BOLIVIA BREAKS OFF DIPLOMATIC RELATIONS WITH
AXIS POWERS.

JAPANESE EIGHTEEN MILES FROM SINGAPORE.

TWENTY-TWO

You either had to wait for a funeral before your turn came to go into the sanatorium, or hang on till someone got better, and Leonard wondered how many did that these days, though he was glad Ivy wasn't considered too far gone while waiting for a place. She had stepped up her appetite and was more cheerful, which may have been because Sophie had left him. At least they thought she had. She went out one night before Christmas and hadn't been seen since.

Her absence might have been less painful if she had taken the children, though it would still have been pain of some sort, but maybe she knew that since they stayed she could come back whenever she liked. Luckily there were only three, because Gilbert had gone to his father. Now that he was fourteen and could work he would have more freedom there. To send the others to an orphanage would have been wicked. They lived here, and would for as long as they weren't too much trouble.

Without Sophie they were subdued, as if grateful he hadn't booted them into the street. None wondered where she was, or mentioned her. Maybe she had abandoned them so often they didn't care who they lodged with as long as they had enough to eat and weren't much bullied. Even Norma helped with the pots and making of beds.

Alone at night it was harder to keep the anguish away, no kids to be glad at what led him to give them more time. He no longer needed to speak his thoughts to know what really bothered him, and silent repetition sharpened their edge. The torment of wondering where she was pierced more destructively than the fact of her not being with him.

She pushed the door open and called her name in the sort of bright voice that expected a rough welcome. It was an evening when he hadn't thought about her all day, which should have indicated that she was in the offing. She kicked snow off her shoes against the scraper, shook coat and scarf by the scullery sink, and came in as if back from pleading at the corner grocery for something off next week's rations. 'It's wicked out there.'

Well, it would be, at the tail end of January, though Harry and Paul had cleared a path between the door and the lavatory, where a tiny oil lamp burned day and night to stop the pipes freezing. Speeches he had composed would not come to mind, except: 'What's this visit for?'

Paul stood with a groan. 'I'm going out.'

He was sometimes happy to let Harry follow him around. 'Can I come, our Paul? I want to see if my blackout button still shines in the dark.'

'Not tonight.' He took the flashlight from the shelf. 'I'll take you to the pictures on Saturday, though.'

'Don't go wasting the battery all over the place.' Leonard was angered at the reason for his going out. So was Sophie, though greetings for her own children were neither given nor expected. 'And don't be back late, either.'

Her smile promised laughter, or a stream of bitter words, he couldn't tell, but would soon enough. Her hair had been permed into neat dark waves slanting across her head, face well made up with powder, lipstick and rouge. Under her usual navy-blue coat a string of jet beads crossed the white jumper to show off her figure. A fawn skirt went down to fully-fashioned stockings and buttoned brown shoes stained from the snow. The leather handbag was also new.

'You don't have much to say for yourself,' he said.

'Oh, I've got plenty to bleddy-well say.' She tapped her breast with an angry gesture. 'But I have to keep it locked in here.'

'I expect he threw you out, whoever he was. If so, he's got more sense than I ever had.' But he added to himself that he must have been a lousy swine to do it in such weather. He also had money, to judge by the new clothes she couldn't have had coupons for. Maybe he owned a shop, or did some business on the black market. Whichever way, he was rich enough not to put up with her carryings on. He let his thoughts out, knowing he shouldn't, thinking he would only be satisfied if he strangled her.

She looked up at the door slamming as Paul went out, unhappy at Leonard forcing her to recall the last few weeks, yet glad to clutch again at their passionate excitements and unforgettable wonders. She had been drinking on her own in The Velvet Glove, and a man said in a nice posh voice that he would like to buy her the next one. She usually stood with Maud, but her husband had come home on embarkation leave. 'All right, duck, thanks, I will.'

Instead of going to a cheap bed and breakfast he had taken her by car to a hotel near Mansfield and booked a great big room with a bath in it. He was good to her. He made promises she knew he could hardly keep, but promises like that were better than no nice talk at all. He made sure she enjoyed herself in bed, what's more. They only got out to go down for a meal. He was about fifty, and bald, but had a nice moustache and wore a gold watch on a chain. It was nothing to do with her where his money came from. He wanted her to stay longer, and she thought she would, especially when he offered to let her live in a flat in Sheffield. Going down to the bar alone because he was still putting on his tie, she got talking to a handsome Polish officer in the air force. When her bloke came down and saw her – he must have been looking from behind the tall plant pots to see what she had got up to, not being as daft as she'd stupidly taken him for – he wouldn't have anything more to do with her. He went bleddy mad, and threw her bits and bobs into the corridor, calling her deceitful and a tart, and other rotten names. She hadn't meant any harm at all, and could tell he was sorry because he came down again to the bar when the Pole had gone and pushed ten quid into her hand. After that she went with so many men she didn't know who she went with. Or where, for that matter. Her lips thinned in contrition. 'It's you I want, and nobody else.'

Who was he? Leonard had a vision of murdering the man she thought so fondly of in her gloomy silence. Faceless or not, he would gladly kill him. 'Or maybe there was more than one?' Revenge would mean taking on every man she had ever known, and he wouldn't live long enough to track down even one. A comforting fire burned, they had all eaten, and the weather kept them safe from German bombers.

'It's not true.' She was close to laughing. 'What the hell do you take me for?'

Well, it might have been. 'I wish I knew.'

Hoping he had little else to say she took a near full packet of Players from her handbag, then looked around to check that everyone was in their allotted place. 'Where's our Ted, then?'

'He's gone to the pictures,' Norma said. 'I wanted the rotten dog to take me, but he's meeting a wench, I expect. He's ever so tight-fisted with his money.'

'He nicks it all,' Harry said. 'He gave me a shilling last week, and winked at me,' at which Norma told him to shut his flapmouth or she would put her fist into it.

Leonard couldn't regard Sophie's return as much use to the house, and when he said so she blew cigarette smoke across. 'You loon, I live here, don't I?'

'Do you? I sometimes wonder.' It was easy to put on a puzzled look.

'I did the last time I was here.'

'It's nice you thought so.' He couldn't understand why he was glad, rancour impossible to maintain, such was his desire for happiness. He had never seen her so smart and lively, all he could want in a woman's appearance, though he would be damned if he would take the rest of what she was in order to pay for it. 'There's no sense in your coming back here.'

'Why isn't there?'

We had got used to living without you, which he thought no one would find difficult once she had left. But he pitied her. 'Because I've had enough.'

'Not as much as I have. I want to live with you and my kids, and not get pushed from pillar to post. Everybody treats me as if I was shit, and I'm not. I'm as good as anybody else, if not better. I'm fed up with it, though, honest to God I am.'

'You should have thought of that before.'

Many a time she had done enough by one hasty move to ruin her life, till there was no point bothering any more. In any case it never took much to convince a man you'd spoilt everything. She began clearing the table, more to draw his justifiable anger than help in the house. 'I always did, but

I couldn't help myself. I thought I would like a bit of fun, that's all.'

He scoffed. 'Is that what it's called?'

'It's all right for you to talk, but you don't know what I've been through in my life.'

His laugh was not altogether cynical. 'It don't look that bad to me.'

'I mean, before now.'

'Why don't you tell me about it, then?' She might feel better. But she didn't, couldn't or wouldn't. He knew how right she must be, but answered: 'We've all had something to put up with in our lives' – and laid a hand on her wrist. 'Don't clear the table, Norma can do it. Just sit down.' What he wanted to say, all of it vile and maybe unjust, was running out of his mind like sand from an egg timer, but piling itself in the bottom half, to be tipped up and fall down again another time. She wouldn't go because he wouldn't let her, though he couldn't say it in case she felt too much of a welcome. 'I can't stand you going off with other men, that's all.'

'I don't,' she said.

'Or telling lies.'

Norma finished wiping the table, brushed away a strand of reddish hair. 'Don't get jealous, Len. You're always jealous, these days.'

He stood over her. 'If you say that again I'll paste you so hard you'll be in bed for a week, you cheeky little madam.'

She whitened with fear, knowing that even a word of regret at what she had said would bring his fist down.

'And it'll serve you right.' Sophie put her arms around his shoulders and kissed him. 'Take no notice, duck. You're one in a million. I've never had such a good man as you.'

Back in her warmth he was certain she meant it. They sat by the fire wondering about their lives, smoking cigarettes and drinking tea. 'I've been thinking things over, about the house.'

He was on the alert. 'Oh, yes?'

'I saw a nice place to let this morning, when I was walking. It had lovely bay windows and a little yard at the back. The agents said we could have it for ten bob a week. It's got more rooms than this bug-eaten dump, and wouldn't even need painting. Me and Leonard deserved something like this, I thought.'

It was pleasant to hear her interested in other matters, but moving would be an upheaval, however easy she said it could be done. On their way upstairs he agreed to look at the place in a day or two. Somebody might have taken it by then.

When they were in bed he said to her: 'I love you more than I've ever loved anybody in my life.' You cow, you vile whore, you tormenting bitch – following in one heart's breath.

'I love you, as well,' she said. 'You know that, though, don't you?' She turned her back to him and lifted her nightgown so that he would do it from behind, and when she came she cried out – he told himself – like the trollop she was, so that he didn't even go to sleep with the peace that was supposed to come with understanding.

HEADLINES XVII

TWO THOUSAND CIVILIANS KILLED IN BOMBING
OF MANDALAY.

FIRST BOMBING RAIDS ON INDIA.

ONE MILLION MORE CANADIANS THAN IN 1931.

US FORCES AT BATAAN SURRENDER.

MR LITVINOV CALLS FOR SECOND FRONT.

FRENCH ATTACK GERMAN HQ AT ARRAS WITH
HAND GRENADES.

KING GEORGE AWARDS GEORGE CROSS TO MALTA.

TOKYO BOMBED.

HITLER RECEIVES TITLE OF SUPREME WAR LORD.

TWENTY-THREE

Smart young ATS women crewed the battery of Bofors ack-ack guns on the recreation ground, and Leonard could not but smile as he and Sophie went by arm in arm towards the river. Even on Sunday the town's defenders were ready, though lately there hadn't been much beyond a blather of gunfire at a lone plane straying from raids in the south.

The change of house had gone more easily than he had expected, the high-laden handcart pushed by Ted, or sometimes both to stop an avalanche of chairs and pots onto the street, even Sophie and Norma doing what they could to help.

He paid the toll at Ha'penny Bridge and, apart from an aeroplane going low, you would think the world was at peace, at least on the country bank of the river. But in Occupied Europe the Germans were murdering innocent people. 'I just can't understand such wild dogs.'

'We're winning, though,' she said as they walked through Wilford village, 'aren't we?'

'We are with the Russians and the Yanks on our side. Even our Paul's joined up,' he laughed, 'so it shouldn't be long now.' Being fourteen, he had enrolled in the Civil Defence Cadet Corps, and did his bit by running messages between sandbagged wardens' posts.

She stared at the brown-and-white cows, placid in the succulent grass, arses shittened and udders full. 'I've always wanted to milk a cow, squirt all that lovely milk into a bucket. I think I'd be frightened, though.'

The scene was real for him, her body big enough for such work. Maybe her grandmother had done it. 'I'm sure you'd do very well.'

'They'd kick me.'

'A lot of Land Army girls have to learn.'

She thought about it, but it made no sense: they were different. 'I'll be glad when the war's over, I'll tell you that much.'

'Things won't be the same when it is' – or so he had read in *The Sunday Referee.*

'I'm fed up with eating powdered eggs and date jam,' she said, 'and spam, and bacon that tastes of fish. And God knows what's in the bread, it's so dark these days. I suppose I have enough to eat, but sometimes I feel clambed to death for summat good.'

He didn't like to hear anybody complain, at least not in the family for which he worked so hard, though he supposed it was normal. 'We're not starving, like some poor souls in France and such places.' Fairham Brook was an arrow of clear water going into the side of the Trent. As a youth he had leapt across the banks of dried mud, and now they went over by the wooden footbridge.

'I'm going to look for another job next week,' she said.

'You don't have to. We can manage on my wages.'

'I know, but if I don't I'll have the Labour people after me.' Work was universal these days, unless you were disabled or had young kids, though he thought she wouldn't be forced to do any because Harry and Norma were still at school. 'I got a letter the other day to say I had to.'

'Then I suppose you'd better.' The piquant smell of herbage from the fields brought back the hiking and biking of his younger days. He hadn't walked so far for a long time, though supposed he must cover some daily miles at work. Between oaks, elms and beeches the air smelled of butter and wheaten loaves, and he wondered in what remote time it was that he had broken the crust of one whose flesh turned grey with the melting butter. 'I love you.'

'Do you mean it?'

He didn't know whether he did or not, but he had said it, so supposed he must. The rich grass helped, and the supple bracken when they walked into the Grove. 'Of course I do.' And he did, if only to get some advantage from the enthusiasm of having said it.

She put a hand on his shoulder. 'I just wanted to make sure.' Her brown eyes looked at him, pleading for something, impossible to know what it was, except that he couldn't give it, unless it was compassion and understanding, wanting him to love her no matter what, accept all that she did until he was destroyed, and could care for her no longer, when she would either die or go to another man and demand the same from him. 'I'll never make you out.'

'Well, I can't always tell whether you love me or not, can I?' He didn't want to upset her. 'If you don't know, how can I?'

'As long as *you* do.'

'Now you know I do.' It was too much of a risk to ask whether she loved him. He only had the strength left for happiness. Leaves lightened by the sun waved in the breeze, to the sound of bees and crickets, a spotted white butterfly – Sam used to know all their names – invisible when it settled. Only in movement was it vulnerable. In a clearing she opened her mouth to kiss him, and they lay on a carpet of yellow primroses and white wood sorrel.

HEADLINES XVIII

GERMANS CAPTURE SEVASTOPOL.

U-BOATS SINK TWENTY-FOUR MERCHANT SHIPS.

INDIAN CONGRESS DEMANDS BRITISH WITHDRAWAL
FROM INDIA.

GERMANS CAPTURE VOROSHILOVGRAD.

RUSSIANS LOSE ROSTOV-ON-DON.

GIPSY PETULENGRO SAYS WAR WILL BE OVER IN A
YEAR.

TWENTY-FOUR

Ted came home from the building site and set a portable gramophone on the sideboard. The case was square and black, and half a dozen records in variously coloured paper sleeves lay neatly behind the stiffened flap inside the lid. The turntable was covered by green baize, and the shining metal head leaned on its solid arm. He stood back to look, as if it were a machine which would perform tricks exactly matching the state of his mind.

Sophie put a cup of tea before him. 'Where's that from?' – implying he hadn't got it honestly.

'I won it, playing cards with an Irish navvy. He was already skint, but I didn't know, so he gave me this, and we shook hands on it.'

His hope of giving them a show they would appreciate was crushed, but it seemed to bother him so little that Ivy wondered what he had gone through already for him to take it so lightly. She saw whoever it was forlorn in his lodgings looking at space where the gramophone used to be, humming the tunes it had played. 'I suppose the poor bloke will miss it.'

'Maybe he will, but he won four quid off me last week, and fair's fair.'

'That's what comes of gambling,' Leonard said, from behind his newspaper.

'You get nowt if you don't,' Ted called back, but Leonard enjoyed the John McCormack records, after Ivy persuaded Ted to give them a tune.

The nine o'clock news was long past, and Sophie hadn't come in from work. Overtime killed home life, if home life it could be called, which he found hard to credit, because the café she served at was shuttered at this hour, as he knew from last night when he had gone at half past ten to look. If she had known of his reconnoitre there would have been an argument, followed by a bigger explosion of *his* wrath because she had been *up to no good*, which was also the case at the moment. Even a battle-royal was better than his spirit gnawing night after night.

If he really wanted to find her he wouldn't know where to start. The pubs his workmates talked about – knocking shops, pudding clubs, red light premises – weren't his territory. Ivy stood at the foot of the stairs. 'Aren't you going up to bed, Dad?'

'Not yet.'

'She won't be in tonight.'

'Who can tell?'

She pressed the hot water bottle to her chest. 'It's just what I think.'

Every time it happened he told himself that he ought to throw her out: ask her to pack up and leave him in peace, push her from the door with boot and fist if she refused, and if he couldn't live without her it would be better to die than put up with this. But the event of her going would make him more miserable than the knowledge that she had gone whoring – he could call it no less – though having his children witness his shame made his heart feel as if caught between colliding coal trucks. 'I'll wait a few more minutes.'

'Well, I'm going up. Goodnight.'

He heard the latch click while setting the table for breakfast: loaf, jam, margarine and teacups, a knife and a plate for each. If he had been in bed, the doors already locked, she could have stayed out with the cats for all he cared. He would behave as if it were the normal time, though if there was such a thing it would certainly be a few hours earlier than this.

'Hello, duck.' She was cheerful enough. 'I didn't know you would still be up.' She stank of scent and gin when he helped her off with her coat. 'If you didn't put the bolts on I could let myself in with my own key. You needn't wait then.'

'I didn't know you had one. Anyway, I like to make sure everybody's in before I lock up.'

'Our Ted had me one made.' She put the kettle on in the scullery. 'Do you want some tea? I do. I'm ever so dry.'

A butcher's knife for cutting the loaf appealed for use: plunge in and twist, like with the bayonet. 'I'm a bit thirsty, as well,' he said, you bag, you whore, you rotten tart. Such sewer-spew rarely came into his mind, so he cursed her for that as well, and loathed himself.

'How much sugar?'

'I didn't know we'd got any.'

She pulled a bag from behind the newspapers in the cupboard. 'I brought this from work.'

'You'll get caught one of these days.'

'They don't miss it.'

'I expect the customers do.' He slid the knife into the drawer like a fragile and precious possession, deciding to say what he thought, no good just asking her not to keep doing it on him with all and sundry.

'I only take a bit at a time.' She came in with two full cups. 'Everybody does it.'

'That's no excuse.'

'It's good enough for me.'

'You,' he ought to say, 'are making my life a misery, when it shouldn't be like that at all. I don't want you in the house, because I've had enough, senseless of me to think we can go on. I don't expect you want to stay, either, though even if you do you've got to clear out.'

The light of her smile suggested misery, which weakened his spite and anguish. 'Even so, it *is* stealing.'

She sat down, a hand around the hot cup. 'Still, it isn't much, is it?'

'I suppose that's true enough.' Nothing would come that he wanted to say, though his heart would burst if it didn't. This was how you felt before having a stroke, and she smiled as if his gaze was a sign of affection. He held her hand, and she leaned to give a long kiss that he had to return. 'Don't go out tomorrow night,' he said.

'All right.'

'Promise?'

She nodded, knowing that only the spoken word mattered with him.

'You mean it?'

'I didn't intend to, anyway.'

'Nor any other night, without me. Will you promise that, as well?'

Such times seemed a long way off, so she would say anything, only wanting him to be happy. 'If that's what you'd like.' She offered a cigarette, never short in spite of their scarcity – an American Camel, this time. 'I must go to work, though.'

'I didn't mean that.'

Having got into the house with so little argument she wondered how long his good mood would last, dreaded a sudden pounding in the face. He hadn't yet done such a thing, but you never knew when he might start. 'I'll cook our dinners tomorrow. We'll have a feast. I'll make a corned beef stew, and that suet pudding you like. Maybe I can get some currants to put in, or some treacle to pour over it.'

They kissed again. 'I'm looking forward to it already.'

She washed in the scullery, breasts low slung but well shaped, soaped the dark hair under arms into a froth, leaned to splash cold water at each. From his stance by the door he stroked her warm shoulders. Putting off the light, he followed her upstairs with an exhausted tread, as if such climbing must go on forever.

HEADLINES XIX

US FORCES LAND ON GUADALCANAL.

SIR JOHN GRIGG ANNOUNCES FORMATION OF JEWISH
REGIMENT IN PALESTINE.

GANDHI ARRESTED. RIOTING IN BOMBAY AND DELHI.

CHURCHILL AND STALIN AT FIRST
MOSCOW CONFERENCE.

GERMANS ADVANCE IN THE CAUCASUS.

TRAIN SERVICE OPENED BETWEEN EGYPT
AND PALESTINE.

MONTGOMERY TO COMMAND EIGHTH ARMY.

CANADIANS IN DIEPPE RAID.

GERMANS REACH STALINGRAD AREA.

TWENTY-FIVE

Unable to sleep, he wouldn't be properly alert while doing his work, but what did it matter if he could not stop her going out to see other men? No battle ever ended: the aftermath grumbled till the next clash took place. He knew for sure she wouldn't change without a disaster that would kill them both. The only way would be for him to change, though even then she wouldn't alter because if he couldn't become somebody else in the first place, and he wasn't sure he would ever be able to – though if you couldn't change you weren't civilised – then that was that. Such self-nagging, impossible to stop, transferred pain to his fingertips.

If somebody wants to do good you are bound to like them, but if they are determined to do bad you can't do anything about it, in which case, why was he so tormented and had no hope of getting to sleep? He was sweating into his pyjamas, a faint snore from Sophie, for which he was glad, because to have her awake would make his open-eyed state twice as bad, though because she was the reason for it he couldn't lovingly stroke her with the motion that sometimes soothed him into dreams.

His fingers spread, drew back from caressing. He loved her, couldn't live if she went away, so would have to endure, even though he couldn't; would have to prevail on her not to go out, care for her by protecting himself first, because he was her only hope and she his.

He would hold himself back longer so as to satisfy her by naming all the cities he could think of. Then she told him he should file his nails. I cut them regularly, he said. She knew men who filed them. She filed her own. He kept his hands clean as well. He scrubbed them every night in hot water. She went with another man, then came home and told him what to do, which meant she was still thinking of that other man. What rooms had she been in that he would never see? What gewgaws and furniture, what carpets and wallpaper fit for her eyes and not his?

He smoothed her shoulders through the nightdress, fingers at the warm flesh of her neck, hands no longer part of him, not sure he had noticed the mole on the left side before – or was it another kind of blemish? – but it didn't stop the press of his fingers.

The wail of the alert signalled a heavy beam suffocating, one of a stockade of trees falling on her. Having been in such situations before, she sent a bang at his most tender place to release the grip.

God commanded that thou shalt not kill, and he said just in time O God what am I doing? the agony of his spirit worse than any she had caused. Her body shuddered at the pain, the room's blackness giving back its shape.

He stopped breathing, to see what it would have been like for her if he had gone on, afraid of himself. Life's air tried to escape its prison but couldn't since he must hold it in even if his brain splashed the walls, a dazzle of light accompanying the patter of a Bofors to scatter the limbs of those in a stray bomber.

She sprang in one movement, knocking the breath from him. 'What was you trying to do, then?'

His body collapsed inwards, a roar of hopelessness ejected. He wanted the comfort of annihilation, a Hill Sixty to go up under him.

'You was trying to kill me,' she said.

He didn't hear, she wondered if he would ever stop, and why he started in the first place, even why he had to when they had gone so calmly to bed.

He turned off the rage as soon as he heard himself, but not out of shame, wanting to smile at the upset and relieve his pain.

'What's all that noise?' Ted put on the light. 'It sounded a real bleddy killpig.'

Leonard's brittle tone pledged violence if they didn't retreat. He should have killed her, and being hanged would have ended it. 'Get back to bed.'

'He was having a bad dream,' Sophie said.

Norma stood by her brother. 'Was he getting on at you, our Mam?'

'Don't be so daft.'

'He'd better not,' Ted grumbled.

'Clear off, both of you, or you'll get my fist.' The light was out, but her eyelids were pasted apart as she wondered whether or not to get up, pack what she could of her belongings, and leave. The older she got the more she had found that all men were the same, and now she must begin to wonder about Leonard.

He was snoring so couldn't hear what she was saying to herself. When she neighed with amusement at the thought he sat up straight. 'What were you laughing at?'

'I wasn't, duck. You must have been dreaming.'

'I suppose so.' He went back to sleep, and so did she.

HEADLINES XX

US TROOPS TAKE OVER GALAPAGOS ISLANDS.

LAVAL DISMISSES GENERAL DE ST VINCENT FOR
REFUSING TO ARREST JEWS IN UNOCCUPIED FRANCE.

TWELVE AND A HALF MILLION POUNDS A DAY SPENT
ON THE WAR.

FIGHTING IN THE OUTSKIRTS OF STALINGRAD.

ADVANCE RESUMED IN MADAGASCAR.

SWEDISH ELECTION RESULTS IN TOTAL REJECTION OF
CANDIDATES IN SYMPATHY WITH THE NAZIS.

NEARLY FIVE HUNDRED SHIPS BUILT IN ONE MONTH
IN THE USA.

HITLER SPEAKS TO NAZI PARTY AT SPORTS PALAST IN
BERLIN.

TWENTY-SIX

Two feet long and flattish, ten inches wide and painted black: the clasp-latch came down over a fixed bow held in place by a simple lock. Because there was never a key in sight he was curious to know what was kept in it. After he had tried to strangle her – which she hadn't mentioned since, as if such an event had been common in her life – she didn't go out at night unless he was with her, and he almost wished she would so that he could open the tin box in his own good time.

You could stay clean of sin when there were neither necessities nor temptations to go from the wayward path. It was easy then. He had always been aware that vile intentions should be fought, but maybe he was growing closer to his real self at last, and only an hour remained before she got home at six, giving time to find the key, and search the box that was visible whenever he reached under the bed for the pot. If she carried the key in her handbag he would never be able to open the box without risk, but he knew enough about her to assume she would hide it in the house for safety.

He looked behind piles of newspapers in cupboards to either side of the fireplace. At the back of his dozen books was a fruity acidic odour of blackclocks whose nest he would eradicate with powder. A jamjar of keys had none of the proper sort, though some belonged to Sophie, obsolete rights to various past ventures he didn't care to think about.

He opened every drawer of jumbled clothes, hoping a stray rat wouldn't bite through his fingernail. In the parlour he pulled mats and rugs out of place, lifted plant pots, vases, the clock.

She had the key with her, so he would give up till a day when she didn't. Or maybe he would forget the idea because he couldn't recall such trembling in his hands. One eye saw what was before him, the other keeping a vision of the street should Sophie turn in from the bus route.

A further look at the box upstairs showed the label on the side signifying one possession which belonged to her alone. Placing it on the bed, he rattled the lock, knowing there was nothing to do but put it back, and hope she wouldn't notice fingermarks on the dust, though more would settle before she got to it.

Noting the exact position on sliding it back, a small key must have been under the middle of the box all the time. The key to the door when left outside the house was often covered by a doormat, a favourite hiding place, which every thief would look under if he knew his trade, though he'd do better than to bother with such poor dwellings as these.

He decided to leave her secrets intact but, unable to say how it got there, the box was on the bed again. After a while looking at it he smoothed a space on the blanket to lay each item down in the right order for putting back.

She had paid out on an insurance policy at two shillings a week so as to get buried with the proper honours, and also to leave a few pounds to her children. A couple of brass bangles and a string of beads had been flashed from time to time, and then there was a gold ring with a diamond he had never seen. Two laundered lace-edged handkerchiefs smelling of stale lavender had her initials embroidered in blue. In the next packet he found a wad of five-pound notes interleaved with pound and ten-bob notes, counting up to three hundred pounds, nearly a year's wages in somebody's language. He smoothed them back, as well as ten golden sovereigns in a little cloth bag, and two colourful cigar bands from Cuba – mementoes of what he didn't care to wallow in. Certainly they hadn't decorated anything Charlie had smoked.

Most of her wages, except for a few shillings to buy lipstick and powder, fags and fares, were given in for housekeeping. He preferred not to think where such money came from, holding up another envelope which spilled out a marriage, and birth and death certificates, as well as old rent books and Christmas cards. He had come upon her family office.

One certificate concerned Clarence George Waterall, son of Sophie and Charles, born in 1932, and another was for the same person killed by a motorcar in 1938, such creased papers they were easy to refold. The worn photograph had been enlarged from a class portrait taken at school. The boy had fair curly hair, forlorn eyes, and a forced smile as if given on command because even at that age it wasn't natural for him to be happy. A jacket over his jersey had no buttons except for one at the neck. Leonard felt such pity for Sophie and her poor kid that he almost did not want to go on living. The death of a child was hard to take. The helpless and innocent fell so that the guilty could go on living. He turned the lock, and set the box with the key in its place under the bed.

The cigar bands on the floor by his foot would be clear proof that somebody had been at her things. In no hurry, he opened the box again to replace the bands in their envelope. He didn't hear the front door click, nor footsteps on the stairs. In the shunting yards preternaturally sharp ears blocked him off from the real world, and did so now.

TWENTY-SEVEN

The afternoon light lengthened her face, beads of water on her coat collar. She had come up in her outdoor things because the light in the bedroom was visible from the street. He had also left the stairfoot door open.

'I never thought you of all people would snoop like that.' She sat on the chair. 'I thought my box would be all right, and that you'd never touch it.'

'It is all right.'

'It don't look like it to me.'

Any excuse would be a lie, but he would have traded much for a convincingly good one. He locked the box, left it on the bed so as to give himself the relief of sliding it underneath when her excoriations began. 'I'm sorry.'

She slapped his hand away. 'You might have left it alone, though.'

'I know. You're right. You don't think I took anything out, do you?' That would have been a very rum act indeed but then, maybe she trusted nobody in the whole wide world.

She sat as if not knowing what to think about that. Her face had become thinner in the last few weeks, lines at her eyes and on her pale forehead. 'That money is my life's savings. I put every penny of it by.'

They faced each other on the bed, neither making any move to go downstairs. 'I'm sure you did. That's what I told myself.'

She pulled off her headscarf. 'I suppose you saw that about our Clarence?' As if glad of any opportunity to mention his name she went on: 'I never stop thinking of him, day and night.'

He fought away the tears of guilt and pity, took a cigarette case from his waistcoat pocket. Pulling two from under the elastic he lit them with the lighter made in the engine repair sheds. 'He looked a nice young kid.'

'He was an angel. He didn't talk much, and he always did what

I told him. God could have taken any of the others. Strike me dead for saying such a thing. But no, it had to be him.'

'How did it happen?'

Her hand shook as she puffed at the cigarette, and he was glad to have smoke stinging his eyes. 'He ran straight out into the road,' she muttered. 'I can't think why. He'd never done it before, because I always told him to be careful of the traffic, and always cross on a Belisha beacon. I drilled it into him many a time, but it did no good. I'll hate that driver forever.' She held a corner of the sheet to her eyes. 'Why did God take a child like him? That's what I'd like to know.'

'It's only the best He wants.' He let her talk, till he broke in to say: 'I won't look into your things again. I shouldn't have done it, I know.'

'Somebody was bound to, sooner or later.' Her normal irritation lessened his painful gloom. 'As long as it wasn't Ted. He would have taken the money and gone out to spend it. He used to do things like that even when he was young. Charlie did, as well. I've lost everything, more than once. That's why I got a box with a lock and key. Them boggers would have ripped it open with a chisel if they'd found it, but luckily they didn't think to look, since I took to hiding it. Their sort don't: they just hope things come their way. I know them right enough. But why can't people treat each other right?'

They have to be taught how to do it, he thought – not certain she would find that a good answer in view of his own behaviour. 'Maybe you'd better let me put the key on my watch chain. I promise it'll be safe there.'

'Yes, all right.' But she made no move. 'Norma was looking after him that day. Clarence ran, before she could do anything. I don't know what to think, even now. She's never talked about him since. She didn't even come to the funeral, but that was because Charlie took them to the pictures, thinking they might cry at the graveside, and that wouldn't be good for them. I can't think where he got such ideas, but he didn't come to the cemetery either because he'd always said Clarence wasn't his child – the bleddy liar. Me and Ted was the only ones there.'

The vacancy in her eyes and voice could never be filled, and the fear in him of having disturbed what should have been left alone gave a similar anguish. Such fear, always ignored, had turned her into someone unknown to him, her or anybody else. 'It was all my fault,' she said.

'How do you mean?'

'Oh, when Clarence was little I was getting ready to go out, and heard him crying in bed. So I went up to bring him down for a few minutes and comfort him, and I fell on the stairs. I only bruised my legs and shoulders but he bumped his head all the way to the bottom, and when I picked him up I thought he was dead. Charlie had gone out already so I ran through the streets with him in his shirt to the hospital. It was summer and still light. They told me he'd got concuss . . . or something.'

'Concussion,' he said.

'That was it. Afterwards, he was a bit slow, though the doctor said it would be all right in a year or two. That's why I drummed it into the others never to let him out of their sight.'

'Well,' he said, 'it still doesn't seem to me as if it was your fault.'

'I was going out to meet a man, and that was all I could think about. That's why I slipped and dropped him. It was God's punishment, I couldn't help but think.'

She wanted him to disagree with her, but he couldn't. God moved in ways nobody could fathom.

'And then the worst thing of all happened, because I couldn't change myself. And I still can't.' She turned, her blouse wet with tears. 'I've only got you. You've got to be good to me, duck.'

'I'll try. I do try, you know that,' though doubting he could make much difference to such grief as this. 'I'll always do what I can.'

'I know you will.' She pulled him close, locking him deeper into her misery with a kiss that might nevertheless improve life for them both. They hadn't been together for a while, and now she needed him. He pressed her onto the bed, and she drew him down, keening with unhappiness.

They sat till it was dark, hands together, then went to the kitchen because the children called up that they were hungry.

HEADLINES XXI

GERMANS CHAIN BRITISH PRISONERS TAKEN
AT DIEPPE.

THIRTY-FOUR NORWEGIANS EXECUTED.

US ARMY TO REACH SEVEN AND A HALF MILLION
MEN BY 1943.

HITLER SAYS BRITISH COMMANDOS LANDING
IN EUROPE TO BE SLAUGHTERED TO THE LAST MAN.

CALL-UP AGE FOR MEN IN UK REDUCED TO EIGHTEEN
YEARS.

BATTLE OF EL ALAMEIN BEGINS.

CHURCHILL ADDRESSES THREE THOUSAND MINERS IN
LONDON.

TWENTY-EIGHT

Even the birds couldn't fly, thrown against the slates of the pavilion, or trapped in bare twigs and branches. Factory smoke beyond the bridge was horizontal, and three stalwart starlings patrolled the park lawn searching under the soil for worms.

Leonard pulled his topcoat collar up, though the gusting westerly was warmish and damp, sun occasionally flooding to encourage the birds. Leaves moved along the ground, quick and erratic, once green but now khaki, advancing like soldiers under crossfire. Most lay in heaps and never got to whatever cunningly concealed earthworks they were trying to reach, but then a few score would join the forlorn hope and tumble forward, lie still, and move on again.

Mud underfoot along Shortcut Lane made him wonder why after his weekly scald in three inches at the public baths he wore his weekend suit, had polished his boots to match, and shaved so carefully with a cut-throat that for once he hadn't nicked himself. The reason was to feel different from his weekly self, and an attempt to clean out the stables of his mind.

She wasn't in the pub on the corner of the street, but then, she wouldn't be, would she? He strolled into every jumped-up pot-house and beer-off in town yet wouldn't come across her. Tom Bosely who pencilled facts and figures into a penny notebook told him there were three hundred and sixty public houses in the city limits, and as many as half again in a ten-mile radius: five hundred in all.

Weeks could be spent traipsing his feet off and he wouldn't find her, and if he did there would be another grand blow-up. She could always be in the next pub ahead, or the one he had just pushed his expectant face into, but searching gave him something to do and thereby calm himself. He ought to be cleaning the cellar or tidying the neglected house, but a demonic engine in his backbone sent him between puddles of black water, stopping at a drier part of the path by the allotment gardens to fasten a bootlace.

Fat clouds wondered whether the city was worth watering and, looking over the hedge, he saw Albert Grindley pulling robust potatoes out of the claggy soil, folded almost double as he walked up and down the rows, a black and white mongrel yapping behind like a rag he'd trodden on.

'It must make a change from oil and train smoke in the engine sheds,' Leonard said, 'being out here.'

Albert stood straight, an old waistcoat hanging open, striped collarless shirt fastened with a stud, trouser-ends tied around the top of his boots. 'Going to a wedding? Or are you just out for a stroll?'

Wind in the trees softened the rattle of truck couplings and the bump of machinery from the colliery across the stream. 'That's about it.'

'The day's good, any road up.' Sweat beads showed on Albert's pink skull between strands of black hair. 'Shurrup, you bleddy ha'porth,' he bawled at the dog.

'Good weather to dig for victory, as well. I used to keep an allotment.'

'Oh ar? Where was that, then?'

'Up Sneinton Dale,' Leonard said.

'Soil's a bit dry there, in't it?'

'You had to water it a fair bit in summer, but I enjoyed it. It got me out of the house every day or two.'

'You don't have it now, then?'

'I packed it in when the wife died.'

'Ar, well, I suppose you would, wouldn't you?'

'I used to take her and the kids there of a Sunday because the air was nicer. We'd make a pot of tea on an old primus stove, and slice up the cucumber in a dish of vinegar. They were peaceful times. Happy as well.'

'They'll be back,' Albert said. 'They still are peaceful, though, when you can cut yourself off. I like this patch of a place. The soil's lovely.' He squeezed some through his fingers. 'Pure gold. It always is near a colliery. And there's plenty of water from that brook across the way. And not only water: the handful of cress I took home from it last week tasted a treat. I couldn't spread the best butter thick, though, like we used to do. Well, you can't with the rations we get.'

'I might look out for another allotment myself some time,' Leonard said.

Albert unwound a bundle of rough twine along a dugover bed, and scooped a furrow, bombing seeds in. 'It might not be easy, but you could be lucky. The stuff you take home helps the table, so everybody wants one. There ain't much in winter though except cabbages. A neighbour of mine keeps rabbits in the backyard. Not supposed to, but nobody says owt these days. I give him all the spare greens, so he slips me a nice fat bunny now and again. They taste a treat in the pot.' The dog sniffed its way into the next garden plot. 'Celery! Come back here, or you'll get my boot up your arse!'

'*Celery!*' Leonard laughed. 'Is that its name?'

'Well, it's the best we could do. We was going to call him Frosty, because it was white-over when I first saw him. He was only a puppy. Some heartless bogger must have got rid of him because they was too mingy to feed him, and he followed me home. Or perhaps it'd been bombed out. Now I think of it he did have a bit of shellshock. He jumped a mile whenever a door banged. The guns don't go off so much now, but when they do we have to put a sackbag over his noddle to quieten him down. My missis wanted to call him Blitz, but I didn't think that sounded right. Then it got distemper or some such complaint, and we thought he was going to peg out. We tried everything, from Bob Martins to Aspros, but one day I came in from the allotment with a few sticks of celery and I noticed his tail wagging like a flag in a gale. I didn't know what it was for a minute or two, then Gwen put the celery to its snout, and before she could pull it away it'd eaten the lot, soil and all.

'In a couple o' days he was as right as rain, so from then on we called him Celery. Just look at the bogger now – his tail starts to shake even when I say the word, eh, Celery?'

The dog looked flattered at being talked about, though the expression suggested it had heard the yarn often.

'Mind you, you never know what he'll eat. He got the top off my tobacco jar the other day, and gobbled up the bit of apple I keep it moistened with. Didn't you, you destructive little bogger?' This was obviously part of the story Celery didn't like, but before it could get clear Albert's well-soiled boot shot side-on, sending the dog with a shocked yelp towards a patch of rhubarb. 'It gets a bit bleak here at times, but Nigel my eldest lad says he'll buy me the wood to build a hut when the war's over. A present for my sixtieth birthday, he told me. A right bleddy pessimist – expecting it to last another three years.'

'It could,' Leonard said. 'That Dieppe raid didn't come off very well in the summer, did it? I suppose I'd better be going, though.'

'Ar, all right. I'll see you at work on Monday. Come on, Celery, let's pack it in and get back home. Happen Gwen'll have a black pudding and a mug of hot sweet tea waiting for us!'

Leonard marvelled, leaving the shady footpath for the road, that he hadn't thought about Sophie for at least ten minutes. Where was she when not harrowing his mind? Maybe harrowing somebody else's. Or she was in bed with he couldn't imagine who.

A green Corporation doubledecker slowed before the post over the bridge. Enraged at Sophie coming back to torment him he razored her picture away as if from an album, glad he could at least run, no longer willing to search for her like a desolate schoolkid.

The last of the queue stepped onto the platform, and veins banged at his temples as if maggots were playing hopscotch. He found a free place upstairs and sat down sweating by an old man with an overflowing bag of large cooking apples on his knees.

The bus trundled behind an army lorry, unrolled canvas showing soldiers lolling in the back, lads like we were twenty-odd years ago, he thought. A pudding-rich smell of curing tobacco came through windows from Players' factory and merged with the rank odour of stuff already smoked in fags and pipes. He lit up to be part of it. They make good soldiers if they don't get killed first, and he supposed Sam was also one by now, though he hadn't heard from him for a while.

A young woman in a yellow frock, hot-blooded in such a wind, pushed a cot along the pavement. People were walking, the bus full to standing, everybody having somewhere to go. He was nearly fifty, and what had he been up to all day? Instead of going to see Ivy in the sanatorium he had been hunting for Sophie, after waiting the whole night for her to come home. He had to know. And so Ivy, watching other visitors, had looked in vain for him. Everyone waited all their lives in vain, but what were they waiting and searching for when all they were likely to expect had already passed them by? Maybe it would be better to *live* for a change, because if you couldn't live, you might as well die.

Ivy deserved more than having to wait in vain. It was only three o'clock, so there was time to collect the bag of toffees, fruit, flowers and handkerchiefs from the parlour table and come back into town to get the four o'clock special from the bus station, which would land him at the sanatorium by half past. What he could not say in the hour before visiting time ended would not be worth saying.

The cemetery through the wide archway in the middle of the almshouses was a forest of stunted headstones, but less neglected than some parts of town. He had kept Beryl's simple memorial clear of weeds and grass, but in the last few years had been there less and less – another cause for regret. Across Canning Circus, as if to keep a watch on matters, were the buildings of an undertakers' place. The city on all sides was a continent occupied by Sophie, and he would stifle if he didn't escape into the world which must exist beyond.

Two old women sat on chairs from their almshouse parlours, and he wondered whether Ivy would likewise be able to get a bit of the sun in her old age.

HEADLINES XXII

ALLIES LAND IN NORTH AFRICA FROM EIGHT
THOUSAND SHIPS.

ALGIERS SURRENDERS.

US WILL HAVE TEN MILLION MEN UNDER ARMS
BY END OF 1943.

GERMAN TROOPS ENTER UNOCCUPIED FRANCE.

CASABLANCA CAPITULATES.

EIGHTH ARMY CAPTURES TOBRUK.

CHURCH BELLS RING FOR EL ALAMEIN VICTORY.

GERMAN SIXTH ARMY SURROUNDED AT STALINGRAD.

TWENTY-NINE

Sophie's shoes knocked the hollow brass fender as she leaned forward to put on lipstick before the oval gold-painted frame above the fireplace. In his working clothes, he watched from the armchair. 'I hope you won't be going out tonight.'

She straightened her lips and pressed them together, liking what was reflected. He also saw beauty there, but couldn't take to it when she replied: 'I don't want to stay in all the time.'

'We can go to the pictures. I don't like staying in, either. Anyway, we don't stay in all the time.' Argue as he might, he knew he had lost, though never stopped expecting to win her, a split too painful to endure but impossible to mend. He could never have foreseen that such a test would be put on him, and if it wasn't all pain, pain at the best of times was never absent. She slept with him as if wanting a few hours of peace which only he could provide, and because he was never able to resist her when she needed to be loved he had to be satisfied with that.

She repainted her lips more carefully, still with her back to him, and said in a bitter tone he could not account for: 'I want some *life*.'

What was life? You got yourself sleepily up in the morning and trusted that the motor of your heart would take you not too harshly through the day. Some dawns were a darker red than others, but he was usually glad to do his work because it never bored him, and hope for a prettier flush in the sky at night. If the choke-smelling smokescreens weren't spread over the city he might even be able to see the stars.

'I want to go where it's lively.' Such a quantity of powder and rouge did her face no good, though he supposed it would make her a bit more visible in dim pub or blackout. 'I want a drink, and a sing-song. I want to talk to people.'

Knowing of no answer that would make any difference, he noticed the seam down the back of her muscular pale legs.

'Where do you always manage to get fully-fashioned stockings?'

She laughed, and it could only be meant for him. 'Oh, you are a bleddy fool, Leonard.'

His moroseness was close to anger. 'I know. I always was.'

'Oh, I don't mean that, duck. But you must be blind if you can't tell I ain't got no stockings on.'

She was right.

'There's a chap at work, he used to be an artist, till the war started – so the silly bogger tells us. Anyway, he takes a pot of paint and a thin little brush, and draws a dead straight seam down the back of us women's legs to make it look like we've got fully-fashioneds on. He charges a shilling a leg – the profiteering dog. But a lot of us have it done, so it must work all right if you don't notice.'

'How can you let a man draw something on your bare legs like that?'

'Well, it don't much matter to a chap like him. He spends the money we give him on scent. I think he's going out with the foreman.'

'I'm still asking you to stay in tonight.'

'Oh, change the record,' she said.

'Or I'll go out with you' – though he was exhausted and didn't much want to.

'No, you won't.' She turned. 'I like to be on my own.'

'I'm sure you do.' In bed together, towards the final moments, when love and tenderness should have blended with the greatest pleasure, his other self silently reviled her, destroying all but the lowest animal enjoyment. Such vindictive moods cooled him into holding the onrush back longer than sweet love would have allowed, for which she was afterwards grateful, as if nothing but love had caused him to bring on her pleasure.

Norma combed her hair over a newspaper, knowing her mother was often generous with her money after she had been out. 'Don't start all that again, Leonard. You're always moaning on at her.'

Ted shoved in his tuppence from behind the screen of his Football Special. 'He's jealous.'

'You pair shut your mouths,' Leonard said.

Sophie clicked her handbag shut, then looked at the clock, deciding she had time to smoke a cigarette before going to her date. 'What a life I have to lead.'

'Well, you aren't going out.' He had said it before, and she had gone nonetheless. 'You can stay in, or we'll go together. But not on your own. I'm fed up living this way.'

'Who wouldn't want to go out every night with somebody like that in the house?' Ted exclaimed.

Norma smiled. 'Let's put on that record, then.'

Sophie was excited at the notion of a night in town. 'I'll be off soon, and you won't stop me.'

Tell her she can take her belongings and her kids and her tin box and not come back. 'I'm asking you to stay at home. I don't see how it can mean all that much.'

'Listen to this.' Ted wound the gramophone, set the needle onto a record.

The same old devilment, but nothing could bruise him any more, *Jealousy* tangoing from the speaker and causing Sophie to smile. He gazed before him, crushing rage as his finger would a reconnoitring blackclock. Whenever he pursued his duty (always mixed with a peculiar love so that he didn't know where the two qualities ended or began) of trying to stop Sophie going to her trade, on would come the record of *Jealousy*, Norma and Ted miming his pain, and pausing only to gauge the effect. The tune dominated him when she was out or he was trying to sleep, followed him down the street, played on the bus, even mocking him at work. Forgive them, Lord, they don't know what they do. But they did. Vicious and irredeemable, they were too well aware, but so rotten that he was strangely able to put up with their torments, the water of such spite dripping so long onto the porous stone of his endurance that the soul had hardened within.

Thinking she saw Leonard smile, Norma said: 'Play it again, Ted.'

Sophie sensed his fury, more dangerous because his body wasn't braced for action. She used to think she was her own worst enemy, until she had kids. 'If you do' – she dropped her fag end into the fireplace – 'I'll break it over your big soft head.'

Ted grumbled that he couldn't even have a bit of fun now, and

Norma looked sour because their goading had come to so little. She was fourteen – a real little bitch, Sophie often called her. But she was to start work next week in a camouflage netting factory, so maybe that would quieten her down a bit. A few nights ago Leonard saw her near the corner shop in the arms of a young lad.

'What are you up to, then?'

'It's nowt to do with you,' she'd said.

'Yes, it is. Get back in the house.'

'You can't make me.'

Words were useless, so he pushed her along. She would hate him even more.

Sophie put on her best coat. She was personable and good-looking but why, he thought, should I pay such a price for that? Well, everybody had to pay something, be it in money or in kind, though whether he could go on affording what it wasn't in him to pay he did not know.

The piece of flesh that lodged in his mouth and was called a tongue would not earn its keep, refused to stir, try to uncurl it as he might. His body would have to do everything, and he stood in the doorway.

'Shift. I'm not a piece of shit you can tread on. I'm not married to you.'

It would make little difference if she was. We live here as man and wife: but he could think of no reason to stop her that she would believe in. 'It's foggy,' he might say, but she knew the streets like someone blind from birth, such as the girl in *The Last Days of Pompeii* he had read. 'It's raining cats and dogs,' but there was an umbrella in the parlour. Even chucking it down with shrapnel wouldn't hold her. Nevertheless, he was too strong for her. 'Take your coat off and sit down.'

Norma set the record spinning. 'Let's play his favourite tune again.'

The pain of his grip electrified Sophie's arm, and she fell into a chair. 'You effing bully.'

A folded hand jabbed out from Ted. 'You're not going to do that to my mother, you jealous bastard.'

Leonard avoided the thrust, his longer reach keeping him off.

But he had forgotten the speed and cunning of youth, and a sally caught his cheek. A hand like a bullet at Ted's chest sent him against the table, which hit the wall with a bang that next door must have wondered at.

She looked on, as if at a play, fists and thumps far off, at what was unreal because she had been there before and knew she could have no effect. Being in a dream, she wasn't able to cross into the iron ring. Then her head seemed to shake itself: 'Stop it, the pair of you, and sit down.'

Ted grappled him at the waist, tangled his feet. He fought every other day at work and knew his stuff, the weight of his knee pressing Leonard's face into the dusty coconut matting.

With his free hand Leonard reached the fender for the heavy-duty hexagonal steel poker, a wedding present from the blacksmith at work. Sophie screamed again for them to stop, meaning me, Leonard helpless as the turntable spun its tinny way, the boxed voice telling him not to use such a weapon, but an order from further off in life overrode the command. Norma came as if to stop the downward lightning stroke, ran to Sophie when the collision with flesh sounded through the room.

Sophie shouted that she would go for the police.

He stood in a corner. 'You can go for who you like.'

Ted, a hand at his face, thought he did not deserve what had been done to him. He had only been protecting his mother, but now she stood aside and didn't seem to care. He leaned against the wall, eyes opening and closing with shock. 'I'll get you for that, I'll fucking blind you.'

A gate clattered next door, a dustbin lid banging as supper slops went in. Leonard wondered how many blows it would take to kill him. He maintained his silence, but he waited, the poker raised. Norma's hand shook over the gramophone, scratched the record on lifting the needle. He wouldn't even forbid her to play. Words meant little with this lot. In the beginning was the blow. Ted was afraid at what he had set free now that blood showed between his fingers. Not as frightened as Leonard was, though being older he was practised in not showing his rage. Heartbeats made his closed teeth feel like rubber.

'Pack it in, do you hear?' Sophie put herself between them. 'I'll go out and never come back if this goes on. All this bother just because I wanted to go for a drink.'

The room was dominated by the measured noise of the clock. Lips twitching, Leonard realised he had missed the nine o'clock news.

'You're laughing,' she said. 'There's nothing to laugh about.'

'He nearly fucking killed me,' Ted moaned.

One more shift from anybody, and he knew he would murder them. Eyes hardly moving from mother to son, he startled them by his words, as if they had expected him to stay mute for the rest of his life. 'You lot would be a pleasure to swing for.'

'He wants sending to Mapperley Asylum,' Norma said.

They would let Ted bleed to death, before thinking to help. 'You'd better get him to a hospital. I don't care if he tells them who did it.'

Sophie put her foot on a spark that leapt from the fire. 'We don't play them games in this family. I'll get some lint to put on it.'

The colour of the room was more vivid, blue and green bands of wallpaper enhanced, the ceiling a lighter pool of white, brown doors reddening. Clock, pots, coats and newspapers were as if ready to get up on legs and move: everything close, and the next moment further apart.

'I'd shop him, if I was you,' Norma said.

'You get off to bed, or you'll get pole-axed as well, by me.' Sophie fetched lint and a roll of bandage from the scullery cabinet, and hot water to bathe Ted's livid gash, more human for having a good reason to stop her going out. 'We don't want no bleddy doctor snooping around here.'

Leonard set the poker in the hearth, hands shaking at nothing to hold, and not knowing where he belonged, though everything familiar lay close, as if he had dreamed of changing houses, and woken to find that he had. Ted swore as Sophie dabbed at his head. Leonard wanted to win the war with them and himself that they had dragged him into, and maybe this little set-to would at least mark the end of the beginning, he thought, turning to wash his hands at the scullery sink.

In the doorway a hoof struck his head, devil or horse he couldn't tell, didn't have time, releasing him into a pool of light. The ballroom of darkness burst, he was bouncing down a mountain slope, hitting every rock, but softly like bumping into wool. Voices spiralled towards him along the tunnel, but he could not get up, drumbeats doubling back from a cul-de-sac and using him as a bridge to walk on. A clap of thunder was a banged door, and the strength in his arm was denied leverage by the rest of his body to let him use it.

THIRTY

Tears marked Sophie's rouged cheeks, but he couldn't believe in such globules of lead. The object of your jealousy was never worthy of you.

She helped him to a chair. 'I wouldn't have credited it. I couldn't do owt to stop him.'

He leaned on his elbow, the icy floor under him. 'Why did I turn my back on somebody like that?' not knowing whether he meant her or Ted.

He's sure it was me, she told herself, but it wasn't. They always say it's me, and it never is. There's nothing I can do about it, shout as I like. 'He shot through that door like greased lightning. A bleddy animal he is. I've never seen anything so quick. He was terrified at what he'd done, though, and so was Norma, because she's skedaddled as well.' From tending one she looked after the other, making a pot of tea, as if it was all the same to her.

He smiled through the pain of keeping his eyes open, at her expression of unconcern. 'I don't want him in the house any more.'

Her cigarette smouldered in the saucer. 'My kids have never been anything but trouble to me.'

'I can see that.'

'Where will he sleep if he can't come here?'

His bruises weren't yet visible under his hair, and he felt no cuts. 'He can doss under at Trent Bridge, for all I care.'

'I know. You would say that, wouldn't you? You're hard, like all men.' She took off the headscarf to wipe her eyes. 'But it's not right.'

Needles of pain shot to his waist when he pressed his neck. How could she know what was right or wrong? 'Norma would have to stay out as well if she wasn't a girl.' The rite of no speech had broken of itself, as it must, and you could never tell what God in heaven would put into your mouth, though it was certain it would always be what you had made up your mind not to say, otherwise how could He convince you that He existed and had power over you?

She put on the nearest expression to a plea. 'I know he's been a rotter, but he can't stay in the street like a dog, can he, duck?'

'He can for me.'

'I'll have to go and look for him. I'm sure he ain't got any money. He needs somebody to help him.' She poured his second cup of tea. 'He's only eighteen.'

'Old enough to be in the army,' he said with some satisfaction. 'He'll be getting his papers soon.'

'It only seems the other day that he was a little lad, like our Clarence.'

'Kids grow up, and the bigger they get the worse they are.' At least yours do, though he wouldn't say it. 'He'll be all right in the army. His sort always is. I just don't want him in the house again.'

'Well, you started the argument,' she said sharply. 'I thought you had gone out of your mind, hitting him with the poker like that.'

'I shouldn't think he would want to come back, anyway, not after that little lot. He should have behaved himself.' They were talking, having something to discuss like normal people, which they hadn't been capable of for a long time. Maybe the fight had been worth it.

'I'd better find him, and make sure he's all right.' She stood. 'I shall have to get the poor bogger somewhere to stay if you won't have him.'

He wondered if they hadn't planned it while he lay stunned, giving her an excuse to go out and not come in till morning. Ted would sneak in after he was asleep, because Sophie would find him in the place they had arranged to meet and give him her key. Leonard might slot in every last bolt, but wouldn't put it beyond Ted to break the scullery window and squeeze through.

'I'm not as hard-hearted as you are.' She adjusted her headscarf and put on her coat. 'You're too sanctimonious. You've always hated him.'

He disliked him as much for what he put Sophie through as

for the pain in his skull, feeling as if only a film of cold water lay between his brains and the air. But it was no use telling her. His own son was in some godforsaken part of the world with the Marines, and he'd never had reason to complain about him. 'You're right. He's been a terror. I don't want to see him again. And if *you* go out of that door I'll batten the place up so that even Old Nick himself wouldn't know how to get in.' He was glad at her hesitation, for if she had gone he would have pleaded for her to come back. 'I only want some peace.' Steadying himself by the table, he was forced to sit again from the pain, rubbed his eyes and temples. 'I'm fed up with leading such a life.'

He was surprised when she sat down. 'Not more than I am. I've been fed up since the day I was born.'

She was unable to help herself, in this and every other mix-up, because she had been in despair since they had met, and even as she said – from the day she was born. But if that was so he wondered why had she come to live with someone with whom she would have even more reason to be fed up? She would have been in the same state no matter who she lived with, and if he had been in a similar mood much of his life, why had he taken her on? The only answer would be to call it love, and ask no more.

Part 2

THIRTY-ONE

In the time it took to get from the book fair at Bedarieux to where I lived the tale of Leonard's War had shaped itself in my mind; but before the heap of paper was written on, in however rough a fashion, months of wrestling with the fluid metallurgy of words would be required. Ideas are ten-a-penny, as a glance at any newspaper will confirm, and only those which come through inspiration make a vivid and moving picture in the reader's mind.

More than forty years later the reality of Leonard's wartime existence replayed itself, so that I had to take care on a road where Dutch and German caravans were almost bumper to bumper on their way to Spain. The planning of the novel took me rapidly to the point where I knew that Leonard Frankland was fighting a war he could hardly win. As history demonstrates – whatever the fanfares of propaganda – there is rarely outright victory in war, and in a conflict between man and woman this is even more the case.

Leonard in his tribulation took some comfort (though not much, all the same) from *The Book of Job*, a large leatherbound volume bought for threepence one Saturday morning in Sneinton Market. Others snared in the inexorable maze of adversity, and consoled by the same text, no doubt included that ubiquitous *Chocolate Soldier*, who realized that an emergency supply of food was more likely to foster survival than clips of live ammunition.

I had met Leonard through my friendship with Paul, and after the pictures we would sometimes go to a milk bar by the bus station to eat cheese cobs and drink tea, where I listened for the remainder of the evening to his anguished monologues. Such talk helped him to bear the weight of living in the same house with a family which I too encountered from time to time and thought little enough of.

If Sophie had known the extent to which two teenagers discussed her she would have been surprised, though not particularly bothered. If Leonard had realised the contempt with which Paul regarded him he would have been mortified. They were the years when a young man is unable to see parents as the parents think he should, after bringing him up with food in his belly and clothes on his back. It is much later that one comes to see their point of view.

The hesitant half-sentences of the young can suggest whole worlds, and invention was also useful in presenting the truth. Whatever didn't occur to me at the time was deduced and used later as evidence for the narrative. Other raw material that came while driving towards the coast – daring only to overtake on the straight and empty – was again forgotten but, once I began to write, most of it returned in due order, inspiration like a dog with a bird of gaudy plumage in its teeth.

HEADLINES XXIII

ALLIES LAND IN ITALY.

JAPAN LOSES A THIRD OF ITS MERCHANT FLEET
SINCE PEARL HARBOR.

SOVIET REPORT ON ATROCITIES IN OREL
NAMES THOSE RESPONSIBLE.

ITALY SURRENDERS.

GERMANS OCCUPY ROME.

MUSSOLINI LIBERATED BY GERMAN PARATROOPS.

VENICE BOMBED.

THIRTY-TWO

Leonard wanted Sophie to come to the sanatorium and fill an hour with him at Ivy's bedside, hoping it would please her to see them as a normal couple at last.

Sophie no longer assumed he wanted her to come so that he would know where she was, though he sometimes made his lack of care so obvious that she didn't believe in it. 'I don't like being in such places.'

He read her mind. In any case it was easier not to care now that Ted was out of the house. 'It's just for half an hour.'

'I'm sorry, duck, I can't. Take Paul with you.'

'He went last week. Anyway, he's playing football with the Cadets.' He supposed she was thinking of when Clarence had died. 'You'll enjoy the ride into the country.'

'I've only got to be on a bus more than a few minutes, and I have to get off and spew in the gutter. You go, and I'll have a nice dinner ready for when you come back. Tell Ivy to get better soon.'

'I'll be sure to.'

The cardboard box was tied with string. 'It's some chocolate and things. And two packets of fags I've saved.'

He smiled. 'You really are a silly so-and-so. She doesn't smoke. None of 'em do in places like that.'

'Well, I didn't know, did I? I'd have a fag even if I was at my last gasp. It wouldn't matter where I was, and nobody would stop me. She can eat the toffees though, I suppose?'

He also had a bunch of white chrysanthemums from Albert Grindley's garden. 'If she don't, she can swap them for something else.'

The natural form of her face had always been broad rather than long, so its painful thinness was more pronounced, the skin stretched, the tone bluish. 'You'll have to fight, and not give in to it.'

She felt a different person already, and kept a smile when the laugh faded. 'What do you take me for, Dad?'

'You'll get better soon, I know.'

She lay back, head against the almost enveloping pillow. 'You can be sure I mean to.'

'She's on the mend, though,' the staff nurse told him. 'We've got her on a special diet. I've never seen anybody eat so much.' Hard to believe, yet he must dig in against pessimism. Three ribs had been taken out below the shoulder, half the lung removed, so there would always be a slightly lop-sided effect when she walked. In six months, the nurse added, she could go home. But what would become of her then? Well, she would be alive at least, though never as fit as others for doing proper work.

He let his tea get cold and, because she had to lie in the vacancy of rest, talked about Ted who in the two months gone in the Royal Artillery had blessed his mother with one postcard. He might already be on active service, but at least he was safe and, for the moment, out of sight. 'I've never liked him all that much.'

The house was also quieter because Norma was at work. In her free time she went out 'to bleddy-well enjoy myself' – absent from the house almost as much as Sophie, who didn't seem too concerned at what her daughter got up to, apart from a rock-bottom order not to bring any unwanted bundles into the house, otherwise she would be slung straight back into the street.

'I've set a rule,' Leonard went on, 'that she's got to be in no later than ten, which she more or less keeps to, unless she tells me beforehand that she'll be at the late-house pictures, and even then I put my foot down if it happens too often.' She would clatter in (but he didn't say this) with a war-like glare as the bolts went on, smelling of scent, beer and God knew what. He was amazed at the antics of mere kids these days, kissing under the unlit lamps before it got dark, and afterwards – he didn't doubt – doing just about everything in entries and alleyways. He was sure a lot of them were no older than fourteen.

Then there was young Harry, coming home battered from school, a rough little lot if ever there was one. Still, he was more amenable than some, and pleasant enough after a stern wag of the finger, though Leonard wondered how long it would be before he got into trouble and was sent away.

Ivy closed her eyes, as if butterflies had settled on them and must not be disturbed. Visiting time was finished, a kiss and caress of her brow. He stood up to leave, encouraged that she had noticed him go, and walked along the avenue of limes to the bus happier than when he had arrived.

The paving of the straight road, woods heavy with rain to either side, looked like the shining surface of a canal. But the bus didn't sink, buoyed by its speed back to town. Passengers who had been to the sanatorium stared ahead or into the green wall of the forest, a few speaking low as if even the glass had ears for their secrets.

He thought of the first ten years after the army when his life had been more or less calm, but decided it was best not to ruminate on earlier times. In any case, when did early times begin, and when had early times come to an end? Early times returned when something took his mind off present misery so absolutely that he did not even brood about how excellent they had been. He wasn't daft enough, or at least not ancient enough, to imagine such times had been all barley sugar, either, though it was hard to believe that the present would ever be looked back on with the same nostalgic glow as those days seemed to have from the present.

As the bus climbed Redhill and went under the high footbridge he lit one of the Senior Service cigarettes that Sophie had put by for Ivy, which lasted so much longer than his normal Woodbine, and to that extent made him feel different.

HEADLINES XXIV

GERMAN TROOPS LAND ON CORFU.

ALLIED AIRCRAFT DESTROY 64 JAPANESE PLANES
IN NEW GUINEA.

14,000 TONS OF BOMBS DROPPED ON GERMANY
IN ONE MONTH.

POMPEII CAPTURED.

MARSHAL BADOGLIO FORMS NEW GOVERNMENT.

OVER 400 CIVILIAN CASUALTIES IN UK FROM
GERMAN BOMBING.

FIFTH ARMY CAPTURES NAPLES.

THIRTY-THREE

The kettle was steaming on the gas, and a heavier tread than Sophie's sounded from upstairs. 'Who's that, then?'

Home from work, there was no dinner on the stove or the hob, and nothing on the table but the cloth. A small hump of pumice on the shelf was for getting the faint dark hairs from her legs before going out, almost a pastime to sit rubbing patiently by the fire. Another was looking at the horoscope page of last Sunday's newspaper.

'It's me, Leonard. I'll be down in a minute.'

He made tea in the biggest pot, as Ted descended in full khaki, beret in his shoulder-strap, a civvy suit and shirt over his arm. 'I want Mam to press me these when she comes in.'

'I thought they taught you to do it yourself in the army?'

'Ah, but she does it better.' His hair was service-short, face ruddy and clean, boots glistening black, belt blancoed and the buckle shining yellow. He looked older than his days, yet more fit.

'The army seems to agree with you.'

The smile was subdued, features back into the old style. 'Ar, but I don't fucking-well agree all that much with *it*. There's too much bullshit from waking up to getting your head down. It gets on my wick.'

'You look well on it.'

'I feel better for being here, I tell you that.'

'They gave you a forty-eight-hour pass, did they?'

He responded with a touch of slyness. 'No, I got fourteen days.'

'In the middle of your training?'

'Well, they think a lot of me, Leonard. They want to put me in for a stripe already. The other lads only got ten days. They had to get rid of us for a bit because they're rebuilding the camp. Salisbury Plain ain't big enough to hold us all.'

Leonard laughed. 'I expect Hitler's shaking in his boots at the news.'

'I don't care what he's doing.'

There was something fishy about it, because Leonard knew the soldiering game. A young chap on his first leave had to be made welcome, however. Sophie wasn't here to do it, which didn't bother Ted much, since he hadn't expected her anyway.

'I want to get these civvies on,' he said, 'and go out for a few pints. The tarts down south think you're no more than a link o' shit if you've got a uniform on – unless you paint a couple o' pips on your shoulder. So I'll change into a proper suit and see what I can do in The Eight Bells. Ah, Leonard, it's nice to be back in good old Nottingham!'

He didn't doubt it. Soldiers were common enough in wartime, but you might not do too badly with a girl if you talked to her properly. He recollected a few nice moments, busy in the kitchen making a meal of powdered egg and strips of fatty bacon, backed up by bread and jam.

Ted sat down. 'Is this all there is?'

'You're lucky to get that.'

'I suppose so.' He wolfed it nevertheless. 'There's a swaddies' club in town where you can get a meal cheap. Any chance of you lending us a quid, Leonard?'

'Wasn't there a pay parade before they sent you on leave?'

'No.'

'There was in my day.'

'It would have meant waiting till tomorrow, so I told them I'd collect it when I got back.'

'Is five shillings any good to you?'

'Keep it. Maybe Mam'll give me summat when she gets home' – thinking what a tightfisted old bleeder he was. He nursed his own thoughts, whatever they were, no word prised out as he sat by the firegrate.

Leonard considered him quiet for a young soldier, never having known one to refuse five shillings before. 'Your mother might not be back for a while. She works late sometimes.'

He didn't seem to hear, his mind far away, until he stood up with the alacrity of a swaddie being brought to attention by the drill sergeant's bellow, neither hand helping him from the armchair. 'I suppose I'll have to go in my army rags then, and look for her.'

The uniform hadn't altered him, after all. Leonard hoped Ted would have more luck at finding Sophie than he would have done.

HEADLINES XXV

CORSICA LIBERATED. FRENCH TROOPS ENTER BASTIA.

POLISH DESTROYER *ORKAN* SUNK BY
U-BOAT IN ATLANTIC.

ITALY DECLARES WAR ON GERMANY.

RUSSIANS CAPTURE ZAPOROZHYE.

PROVISIONAL GOVERNMENT OF FREE INDIA
FORMED IN SINGAPORE.

HALF A MILLION COALMINERS STRIKE IN USA.

BUTTER RATIONING IN NEW ZEALAND.

THIRTEEN THOUSAND TONS OF BOMBS DROPPED ON
EUROPE IN ONE MONTH.

THIRTY-FOUR

When Sophie came home from an all-night stay she passed a five-pound note across the table to Ted, nearly a month's pay for a recruit. How many more had there been? Leonard wondered. 'You'll spoil him.'

'He's only young once. Which is just as well, I suppose.'

Harry sat on the floor in a corner arranging empty cigarette packets into a palisade, boxing himself in, then making a breach from the middle, only to rebuild the fort to a different shape, as if the mechanics would absorb him forever.

Ted slipped the money into the pocket of his civvy jacket. 'Thanks, Mam. I'll do the same for you one day.'

'I can see that time coming all right.'

'Well, you never know. I might win the Irish Sweepstake. My right hand was itching all last night.'

'Where do you get so much money?' Leonard wound up his watch. 'I've never seen so much floating around.'

'I earn it.' Her lips tightened. 'Every penny.'

He had told himself never to ask again, but he had spoken nonetheless. 'There's a name for what you do in the Bible.'

'Is there?' she jeered. 'I expect there is. You're beginning to sound like my father.'

'Well, maybe he had something to complain about.'

'You never knew him, so how do you know? I hated him. We all did. He could never sit still, and was into everything we did. My brother got out, and my sister married a man who went to Canada. I'll never know how my mother stuck him. He was the rottenest old devil as ever walked on God's earth. He kept a horsewhip in the kitchen, and it's a wonder I don't still have the marks on me. I think he must be roasting in hell by now, though I wouldn't know because I ran away at fifteen and never went back. I haven't seen him since. He can be dead for all I care. Not that he was the only man I hated. There was plenty more after that.'

She sat wondering about her life, bemused at having said so much, but irritated with herself for not having said enough to make her feel better.

'Anyway,' Ted called, 'what was it you was accusing my mother of?'

She came out of her mood. 'He's jealous again, always bleddy jealous. Even when I go across the yard to pee he thinks I've got a man in the shithouse!'

'Jealous,' Harry said softly, putting one Woodbine packet on another, and setting his cheek on the floor to gust them flat. 'Always jealous.'

'And have you?' Ted swigged off his mug of tea, thinking it manly to stand up slowly and open the gramophone. 'It's so miserable, we need a little tune.'

'Yes,' Sophie said, 'play us a nice tango.'

He would be going back to his unit in a few days, so Leonard let him get on with it, though felt more and more that there wasn't much left for himself in this house, working six days a week to provide a refuge for people who did all they could to make his life unbearable.

'I heard you arguing all the way up the stairs.' Norma had a blanket over her nightgown. 'I can't even have a lay-in these days.'

Sophie laughed that she looked like the Queen of Abyssinia.

'You should get up earlier,' Leonard said.

'I work hard at that effing factory, don't I? The pay's rotten, as well. But all this noise: I can't even hear myself dream.'

'It's Leonard, he's getting jealous again.' Ted set down the gramophone head with a gentleness hard to credit with his normal movements, and the song swathed its rhythm through the room, he and Norma exaggerating the Victor Sylvester style, though careful not to send any gewgaws flying.

'I can't help but laugh,' Sophie said, 'at that pair of silly boggers.'

Leonard, at this callous unanimity, pushed his way between, and before either could recover lifted the record off and snapped it crisply into several pieces against the table.

Ted feared to tackle anyone so enraged. 'You're off your head, you silly old bastard.'

He feared he was, but picked up the pieces and dropped them in the grate, he and the others watching as they twisted in the heat. Then he put on his jacket under their silence and walked out of the house, only Harry calling for him to come back and burn some more.

THIRTY-FIVE

An invisible blade of frosty coal smoke from trains and house chimneys cut familiarly at his nostrils as he strode along wanting to damn them all yet knowing that, even so, there was no guarantee of them vanishing this side of hell or heaven, and they would be there when he got back.

He drew his collar up and went along Glasshouse Street. At the Central Market wartime business was slack, a few handcarts forlorn along the pavement, and a couple of tall soldiers in purple berets buying at a fruit stall.

The same thoroughfare became Broad Street (not broad enough) and Stoney Street (merely cobbled); house doors opening onto pavements, and children playing warily, shouts drowning the flick of marbles before they dropped into winning holes.

Among lace workshops and warehouses vans were collecting camouflage netting or parachute material. Every place worked night and day, women and girls keeping the machines going. Hosiery firms turned out uniforms to clothe the serviceman in all climates. Raleigh made shellcases by the million. John Player produced tobacco and fags so that everyone could have a puff in a tight corner, or a relaxing drag in a pub. Boots' concocted medicines for dosing the wounded and ailing. Cammell Lairds made artillery. Tanks were assembled at Chilwell. Something definitely hush-hush went on at Ruddington Moor. Ericssons did telephones and wireless sets. Scores of other factories were subcontracting for bigger firms, the whole city and environs labouring flat-out to help win the war.

Nobody was idle, from fourteen-year-olds to men and women in their seventies. Not since the last big do had there been such scope, and he wondered why everyone couldn't be so employed in peacetime. They might occasionally moan at not having much to buy with their hard-gained pay packets, but there were fairer shares of food which hadn't been possible till then. Pubs had beer, picture houses did top trade, and there was a wireless in nearly every house so that they could even listen to Lord Haw-Haw if they cared to. The country wouldn't go back to what it had been like before, and that was a fact.

Broadway was a short throughway of redbricked factories with their grand entrances up steps, looms busy behind rows of tall windows, sky visible only on bending backwards to see a four-engined plane flying across. A young boy pushing a handcart of planks brushed his shin. 'You want somebody walking in front of you waving a red flag,' Leonard called out merrily enough.

'Bollocks!' – a flash of pale and lively face as his barrow rattled at a greater rate over the cobbles.

'I'll put your bollocks where your batchy head should be.' Leonard, half into a run, struck air with his fists: 'You cheeky little bastard!'

A girl walking by, with a pinched face and hands deep in overall pockets, looked as if he was ready for a straitjacket. He lowered his hands, thinking he could well be, face heated with shame, turmoil, chagrin, fierce heartbeats saying he might be about to bend over the gutter and throw his stomach up.

He quietened such unwarrantable rage, thinking that if he didn't teach the kid manners, someone surely would. Youngsters were like that because they worked hard and earned money. Every evening they came exhausted out of the factories, joshing in the streets before the twenty-mile bus ride home. Up at six in the morning, they caught the bus again, rather than work in the colliery at the end of their garden.

He walked the slippery cobbles wondering where he was going and why, but only heading as far as the next turning, which was the same with Life, because you could never see beyond the limits of your sight, while only God, if such he was, was able to view the pattern from above.

He had a home to go to but couldn't stop walking, waited for an old man on a bike to pass before crossing the road. He didn't know whether he loved Sophie, but you lived with a woman for better or worse, and worse was better than nothing if you loved her and didn't want her to leave. Looking back, she had fallen into his bed so quickly he hadn't known her for what she was.

The only way they could be intimate nowadays was for him to imagine she was someone else.

He couldn't put up with her going off with other men, though he didn't know how to end it unless to hang himself. But he was too tenacious of life, or too cowardly, or too aware that such an act might make certain people happy, or an equal number unhappy, and he didn't see why he should disturb either sort to that extent. And above all, to do such a thing would be the worst sin he could think of.

A few years ago such calculating thoughts had been no part of his nature. It was surely a matter of *know thyself*, in which case you must make the effort to do so more and more, otherwise you ended up at the mercy of those who thought they knew you better than you did yourself, and there was no fate worse than that.

THIRTY-SIX

From a bomb-blasted gap in the houses he looked at a train ploughing boisterously through the marshalling yards under a rudder of smoke, lines of carriages and wagons as if in a shop window of toys before the war. On the edge of the city a power station threw up cloths of steam. The town closed you in, though maybe there was a better life in the wooded hills beyond.

A few feet apart, decrepit façades had curtains across their windows, the glass cracked, brown paint bubbled, putty broken, since there was nothing to sell. He walked down a stepped footway to a street of bombed houses: destruction brought change, though people were killed who had done nothing to deserve it.

On Long Row, women made-up to the nines (some so young you would think they were still at school) strolled up and down calling at any man or soldier going by. One even had a toddler with her, and Leonard couldn't think why. He made a bridgehead at the counter of Yates's Wine Lodge.

'I'd know that thirsty voice anywhere,' Albert said. 'Even if it was in the middle of *The Hallelujah Chorus*.'

'Why aren't you on your allotment digging for victory?' He opened his jacket, at the heat from so many people. 'It's just the right raw day for it.'

'You can't get the spade in – and if you do it weighs half a ton. Mind you, it's lovely to see all them fat worms wriggling about.'

'You could do a bit of fishing.'

Albert detected that something wasn't right, while pressing tobacco into his pipe. 'Life treating you well, Leonard?'

'I'm in the pink. Never felt better.'

'Well, that's all right, then. Mind you, I have thought of a bit of fishing. My youngest lad's just been called up, so I might take his tackle out and see if I can't pull a few tiddlers out of the Trent. They say it's good by the power station, but I reckon there's too many at it. People are bleddy locusts these days. You'd think it was the Siege of Mafeking.' He drew a long suck of his pint. 'Last September me and the missis thought we would go blackberrying. She remembered a lovely spot from years ago near Beeston. Used to get her bloomers caught in the brambles, I expect, when she was courting the bloke she packed in to take up with me. But there wasn't a blackberry to be seen. We ended up with six green 'uns in the bottom of a tin, hands all scratched to boggery. So no jam, even supposing we could get the sugar to make it. It's the same with mushrooms. And the wild rabbits have all been eaten. They'd start on the moggies if they weren't all skin and bone. Still, they feed the lads in the army, so my lot are all right. I've got three serving now. "This is going to be the war to end wars, Dad," my eldest said, "not like the one you pansied about in last time." I nearly knocked his block off, except he's bigger than me. And now my only daughter's hopped it as well, into the Land Army. A glorified muckraker, I told her. She nearly chucked the teapot at me.'

Leonard called for another. 'The house must seem a bit empty.'

'Seem? Me and Gwen rattle around like French pennies in a gas meter. Whenever she wants to shout at me I'm not there. Mind you, when I want to give her a kiss, she is. We might take a couple of lodgers, and make a bob or two. It'd be company. No use getting a smaller house, either, because my mob'll be back when they've won the war.'

'If you aren't careful,' Leonard said, 'you'll get some soldiers billeted on you.'

'Not likely. If the Council people come snooping I'll grab a few kids off the street and chuck 'em in the beds. God knows, there's enough around our way, and most of 'em don't know who their fathers are. One or two darkies, as well.'

'How many rooms have you got empty, then?'

Albert laughed. 'You want one?'

He wondered, for a moment. 'Have the next jar on me.'

'I thought you was serious for a minute. I've got two, if you know anybody respectable. That'll leave one for when my lot comes on leave, and if they all show their clocks at the same time they can fight for it. They would, too. They're demons when they're together. Yes, I will have another. I like the ale in this place. Even Gwen don't mind me coming here, though I think she'd like it a lot less if she saw all these tarts.'

Leonard felt better with a couple of pints in him. 'Where do they go when they pick somebody up?'

Handsome ebullient Americans filled the place with their accents. Albert joked: 'I didn't think you was like that,' and saw his mistake. 'Well, I suppose they take 'em home. The parents don't care these days, being partial to some Yankee fags or a tin of their posh snap. Or there's all them bed-and-breakfast places up Mansfield Road. Six-and-a-tanner a night, or so I heard.'

Leonard walked tall and upright towards home, mended somewhat at knowing he had a few pounds in his Post Office book and could lodge with Albert while looking for a place – if he had to.

THIRTY-SEVEN

Sophie was in the scullery cooking dinner. 'I thought you was never going to come back.'

He was jovial. 'You missed me?'

'I always do, you know that.'

He kissed her. 'That's good news.'

'It don't come from *The Daily Liar*, either.'

'I'm glad you say so.'

She smiled. 'It wouldn't pay me to believe anything else, would it?'

He hung his scarf on the back of the door. 'Wouldn't it?'

Sophie was two women, but he lived with one at a time, and the one he didn't like could not be turned out of the house without taking the half he was in love with, which he was sure loved him. Because of this she made him feel he was two different men, and if he was, neither of them could manage the part of her that he could not endure.

She stood up from the oven. When she stayed home she cooked, and looked after things, so what more did he want? Couldn't she do what she liked with herself? 'So what's wrong with you now?'

If she didn't know, she lived in an unthinking world, and if she did she was being callous. 'Lots of things.'

'Don't you think it's time you stopped pulling such a meagrim every time we're together?'

He told himself the same every morning when shaving. If it wasn't good for her to see his face it was even worse for him. Responding to such a direct attack wasn't easy at the best of times. The features he saw in the mirror were becoming less and less familiar.

Men, she thought, at his long silence. They either hit you or they sulked, and when they weren't out for all they can get they were robbing you blind. 'Talk about Les-bleddy-Miserables! You've got nowt to complain about, as far as I can see.'

He altered his tone to avoid a more bitter quarrel. 'I went for a walk around town.'

She wasn't very interested. 'I hope it did you good. Your breath stinks of ale, so it must have' – glad he was capable of enjoying himself, and didn't only drink when out with her.

'I walked by Long Row, and saw a few others like you walking up and down.'

She turned on him fiercely. 'What's that supposed to mean? I never go there, so mind what you're saying. I only pass it on my way to work.'

'Where do you go, then, every time you go out without me?' He called himself a fool for asking such a question, yet wondered why in all these years he hadn't followed her. He had, once, but she had known how to lose him, proving that she was up to no good, which she had never denied, anyway. If she had positively done so he might well have believed her.

'I go out,' she said, 'on my own business. And it's nothing to do with you.'

'But it has. Haven't you heard of disease? There's plenty around, and posters warning you all over the place.'

Lips were set, but her eyes glowed with amusement. 'I take care of that' – as plain an admission as he had any right to expect.

He spoke coolly. 'I'm not going to have you carry on, and live here at the same time.'

'Do you know what you're saying?'

'I do.'

She took off her apron. 'I'm going, then.'

The smell of her cooking was in his nostrils, saying you can't choose the time for the end, it comes of its own accord. He looked at the wall, and waited silently for her to go. What you wanted to happen with all your heart never came easy. Judging her glance, he sensed the torrent of scorn before her departure.

He wondered at her persistence, courage, gall, at her not knowing what she did either to others or to herself. From standing by the door she sat down to face him. 'Have you got a fag?'

Since she was leaving there was no reason not to be generous. She lit it from her own box of matches. 'I'll tell you' – and by her quiet voice he knew he would be getting the truth – 'I've been on the game ever since I was fourteen. That was the only way I could get what I wanted. The trouble was I didn't know what it was I wanted exactly. I wanted something, and if I didn't get it I would die. So I never got it. But you never do get what you want, do you? As long as I went on trying to get it I didn't feel so bad. Where that leaves me, I just don't know.'

'It seems to me that you didn't get anything at all.'

'And do you know why?' She paused, as if he was so wise that he might. 'No, how can you? It's because too many men have robbed me blind. They knew I didn't know what it was I was after. I knew nothing. I was all mixed up, and still am. It's surprising what the worst sort of man soon knows about you. The only reason I stay with you is because you don't try to rob me. I don't think I knew any man could be honest before I met you.'

Her confession made him happy. 'It's nice to hear it.'

'I love you, Leonard. I've never loved anybody like I love you.'

Funnily enough, even Beryl had never said it to him like this, in so many words, thinking – and he believing her – that she didn't need to. Or maybe she had and he had forgotten. They had almost grown up together, so all that they meant to each other could stay unspoken, and that had seemed all right. Yet to hear it from Sophie, surfacing clear and tender through the mess of his existence, lit up his soul with gladness and love, illuminating his wilderness. He spread his fingers over her shoulder. 'Why don't you give up the kind of life you lead, then?'

'I've tried, many a time. But I can't. I know I can't.'

'You can. If you can say you love me like that you ought to be able to do it.'

'I don't want to.'

That was it.

'Not now,' she said.

She wanted everything. She didn't know you had to choose, make the effort and sacrifice of a decision and stick to it. He struck the table with his fist. 'You've got to do it.'

In the scullery, she clattered pots about in her distress. He was like all the rest of the men, telling her what to do. 'You can get your own dinner.'

'Let's talk,' he said. 'Don't get so upset about it.'

'You might not want to rob me blind,' she shouted, 'but you still want to ruin my life, and I don't know which is worse. But I'm not going to let you.'

'If I didn't,' he said, 'you would be ruining mine. That's how it is when two people live together. As soon as you get married you become half a person. But I don't mind, because I'm still as much of myself as not to let it bother me.'

'You're the worst person I know,' she cried. 'I fell for you, but I can't breathe when I'm near you.'

The last words had been said. He had lived with her for nothing. His life was an agony too great to be borne.

She fell back against the wall. 'No, don't!'

Two wicked bangs at the head, and fingers pressing her throat to stop another scream.

Paul came in, and pulled him away. The black dog that had torn its way out would have killed his son as well, but he stood by the table looking at his hands, couldn't remember what she had said to make him act, and because he didn't want to recollect anything he thought it couldn't have been important, a kind of madness that made him passive out of fear.

She went back into the scullery and he heard her being as sick as he had been coming back from France on that rotten old up-and-down boat, cleansing himself of all that he wouldn't care to remember, or so he had thought. But everything that happened went deep inside and rotted the spirit. He sat her down, stroked her hair, talked to her.

'Leave me alone,' she said. 'I'm all right.'

His state of shock had been transferred to Paul's face. 'What were you doing to her, Dad?' He was crying. 'Don't hit her again. Never. Say you won't.'

It had taken place in somebody else's world, or ought to have done. Sophie was better at keeping it out, relit the gas to rescue the dinner, though only looked at him when the meal was on the table, glancing at his still features as if she hadn't known him till then.

He looked for Paul, to say he hadn't meant to, that he was sorry, they were only having a bit of an argument, but he had run out of the house because he couldn't stand it. And neither could Leonard, wanting to follow yet not able to.

HEADLINES XXVI

RUSSIANS CUT GERMAN COMMUNICATIONS
WITH CRIMEA.

US FORCES LAND ON BOUGAINVILLE ISLAND.

SPEZIA BOMBED BY ALLIED AIR FORCES.

GERMAN COUNTERATTACK NEAR
KRIVOY ROG REPELLED.

SESSION OF FRENCH PROVISIONAL
CONSULTATIVE ASSEMBLY.

OVER THIRTY THOUSAND CASUALTIES IN
NORTH AFRICA LANDINGS.

THIRTY-EIGHT

He supposed that Ted, at the end of his fourteen days, would be going back to the army.

'Let 'em fetch me.' He had been out all night, red at the eyes and careworn.

'They will, if you don't go.'

'I hate the army. I can't stand the bullshit.'

Maybe not — he'd be the last to. Leonard held the bread on a toasting fork at the bars of the fire. But what was bullshit? A fanatical attention to cleanliness and order, the discipline of having to do as you were told, self-respect in thought and dress. Like it or not, it was a help in life.

'I mean, what's it all for, Leonard?' He pleaded to know, troubled because he didn't and perhaps never could. 'Honest, I don't see the point of it. I never wanted to go in the army. It's nowt to do with me.'

Leonard recalled his own shock, the drill and training that left you not knowing who you were, though after a while your proper self came back. 'Others have to put up with it.'

He went to work, because whatever happened, and however he felt, his job had to be done, which he didn't mind because he would hardly know what otherwise to do. He would get no money, for a start.

Ted was still warming himself at the fire when he came back in the evening, and Leonard thought a bit of firm advice might be called for, that in fact Ted could well be waiting for some such words to help him on his way. 'If I was you I would get into that uniform and make a move. You'll only be a few hours late.'

'Don't get on at me,' he cried. 'Just because Sophie ain't in.'

So Leonard noticed, the first time she had gone out since their argument. 'They don't like you to be late from leave in the army.'

Ted's laugh was bitter. He was Sophie's son, right enough.

'Leave? I ain't been on no leave. I told them to stuff the army. Don't think I'm the only one, either. Blokes go missing all the time.'

Leonard was alarmed at sheltering a deserter. 'I expect they get them back again, as well.'

'Some of 'em, but not me.'

'I'm surprised the Redcaps haven't been for you.'

He lit a cigarette. 'When I filled in the papers I gave them the old man's address, so they went there. The lousy bastard sent 'em here – naturally. He would, wouldn't he? – but Sophie told 'em she hadn't seen me. "I thought he was in Burma," she said, "and good riddance to him!" Mam's the best liar I know. Anyway, one good turn deserves another, so I wouldn't get on at her if I was you. She's one in a million.'

Leonard had only to call at the nearest police station to get matters put right, which some would find easy enough, but Ted was Sophie's son, and Leonard was living with Sophie, and in any case he didn't think he could do it, which Ted must know, as did his mother. 'You'd still be wise to go.'

'No bleddy fear.'

'How do you think you're going to live?'

The problem seemed to bother him, at least. 'I expect something will turn up.'

'You'll need an identity card, and insurance cards, and you can't get those from the Employment Exchange without a discharge written in your paybook.'

'You can get owt if you pay for it. All you've got to do at these offices is flash a bit o' writing under their noses.'

'I wish you would be a good lad, though, and go back. It's a terrible thing, to be a deserter.' He too had been thoughtless in his life, and whenever he had, such as in going to the war as a youth, and then (it was only with an effort that he dragged it clearly into his mind) having got so heedlessly embroiled with Sophie, he had brought little but pain to himself and those around him.

But Ted didn't need anyone to tell him how to make his way in the world. 'I'm not going, and that's that.'

Such freedom would have to be paid for, and Ted couldn't guess by how much, Leonard knowing that he too would have to share it whether he cared to or not.

HEADLINES XXVII

POLISH MINISTER DETAILS GERMAN
ATROCITIES IN POLAND.

VATICAN BOMBED.

KIEV CAPTURED BY RED ARMY.

SIXTY U-BOATS DESTROYED IN THREE MONTHS.

DE VALERA SPEAKS ON IRISH NEUTRALITY.

AUSTRALIANS USE TANKS IN NEW GUINEA.

RELEASE OF OSWALD MOSLEY ON HEALTH GROUNDS.

RAF BOMB MANNHEIM AND BERLIN.

ALL MALE STUDENTS AT OSLO UNIVERSITY ARRESTED.

THIRTY-NINE

Ivy had gained sufficient weight as hardly to need padded shoulders, but the woman in the next bed had showed her how to stitch them in, and they felt good when she put her coat on and fastened it against the cold she was going into. Rather than a sign of pessimism the problem of fitting the shoulders had given her something to think about when there had been little else to do but rest, read, and wonder on her fate.

'Yes,' Leonard said, while she kissed her friend an affectionate goodbye, 'it's pretty nippy out.'

'How's Sophie?' she asked when they were on the bus.

'The same as ever.'

She didn't like what she was going back to. 'You ought to find another woman, Dad.'

The only answer to such advice was a harsh one, but in the mutual silence he wondered why indeed he didn't make it his purpose to meet someone else, deciding it was because he did not know where loyalty ended and weakness began. Sophie had so little loyalty that he had to have enough for both, so he concluded that, like it or not, he thought too much of her to let her go. 'Ted's home again.'

'I thought he was in the army.'

She would have to be told. 'He came out.'

'But how is he keeping body and soul together, ha-ha! As if I couldn't guess.'

'He's working on that big new ordnance depot near Ruddington. It's work of national importance' – which was the best he could do, such half lies that she must realise the truth.

She wanted to make sure her father knew he was lying. Having been close to death, with so much time to think on either side of the darkening slope, she wouldn't tolerate half measures. 'What you mean, then, is that he deserted?'

'Yes.'

'People like him do.'

He smiled. 'Thank God there aren't too many, or we would have to put up with the Nazis.'

They passed the turning for Newstead Abbey, autumn trees gilding both sides of the drive in glowing copper. 'You didn't desert when you were in the army, did you?'

'It never crossed my mind.'

'Nor our Sam, for that matter. Nor Eunice, either.'

'I'm sure it never crossed theirs.'

'We're different people,' she said.

'I know.' She was more straightforward and talkative now that she was better. Yet she wasn't completely cured, or so they had hinted. Whoever was, in any case? You could never get a proper word out of doctors. Maybe they didn't know. They weren't magicians. So much depended on the morale, as was often said. She wasn't to go to work for a year or two, had got to eat well, and take long walks in the open air.

'You sent me to Sunday School. Remember?'

He held her thin fingers. 'Of course I do.'

'That makes us different from Sophie's lot.'

'I suppose it does.'

'And Sam was in the Boys' Brigade.'

'Well, he liked it.'

'Even Paul's joined the Civil Defence.'

'Even!' he laughed. 'He couldn't wait.' When not out with his mates, or at the pictures, or at work, he sat in his room swotting up on his first aid and hygiene manuals.

'I didn't always like Sunday School, but I'm glad I went.' Raw autumn fields lost their muddy borders in the dusk. 'I'll be glad when I can go to work.'

'There's no hurry. Maybe you'll meet a nice young man to take you to the pictures now and again. You'll have to find an interest in life.'

'Oh, I've got plenty of that.' A hobby? Night school? She didn't want anybody's counsel, because what good would it be from a father who had taken in such a family?

'Anyway,' and he couldn't think why he said this, 'you aren't bothered by the idea of Ted being in the house, are you?'

What funny ideas he had! 'Not a bit. Why should I?'

162

FORTY

'I'd have trimmed the house up like you was back from the war,' Sophie said, 'if I could have found some coloured paper.'

Home was a cold place outside of the kitchen, hard to say she was glad to be back. Being where she had been seemed as if that was where she still belonged: lights in the ward yellowing towards dusk, and certain that during the night she would sleep in peace. She could never be off guard in this so-called land of home.

Sophie laid thick slices of ham on a plate, with lettuce and tomato, and set it before her with a cup of sweet tea. 'Come to the fire, my duck. We've got to look after you now.'

She had no trouble with her appetite. 'Where did you get this lovely ham?'

'Our Ted brought it in, a leg of honeydew for us to scoff.'

To say *our* Ted implied that he was one of us from birth, she thought, but I didn't elect him into the family. 'Isn't ham rationed?' – when you could get it.

'Everything is, except to them as looks for it.' She picked off a string of fat and squashed a piece of bread around it. 'They'll be putting spuds on coupons next, I shouldn't wonder. Maybe Ted won it playing pitch-and-toss. "Ask no questions, Mam, then you'll hear no lies," he said. He's been looking forward to you coming home, though. That's why he got you something nice for tea.'

One slice was enough. 'Would you like the other, our Paul?'

He sat on the sofa, out of their circle. 'I've had some already.'

His cadet uniform was neat and clean, trousers knife-edged. 'Did *you* press 'em?' she asked.

He nodded.

'Aren't you glad to see me, duck?'

'Yes.' But his voice was hard. 'You know I am.'

'Put the rest of the ham in the cupboard till later, then. I'd like some more tea. I get so thirsty, lately. Anyway, why don't you eat some lean yourself?' she said to Sophie.

'I've got a bit of a toothache.' She twisted her lips, turning to Leonard. 'It gave me gyp all last night.'

'There's a dentist up the road. I told you to get it seen to.'

'He'd yank it out. I don't want to be a toothless old hag just yet, so I'll keep dabbing at it with that tincture. It only comes and goes. Like our Ted,' she laughed, holding her face. 'We ain't seen him for a couple o' days.'

Leonard expected him back soon enough. 'Maybe he's found lodgings. I'm sure he'd rather do that than hang on here.'

Ivy was glad he wasn't in. 'At least the Redcaps don't come snooping around any more,' Sophie said.

'I suppose they've got better things to do.' He kept expecting Ted to see that the only course was to go back to his unit and give himself up. When he said as much Sophie's laugh showed the dark area of aching tooth. 'Why should he? He's doing well at his job now that he's got proper papers and an identity card. I know he can be a rotter, but it's nice to see him now and again. He'll be all right with us till the war ends – if ever it bleddy does.'

'What about the neighbours?' Ivy asked.

'What about 'em?'

'They talk, don't they?'

A woman and five kids lived with her sister who worked on the buses, but they minded their own business. On the other side was an old couple in their seventies, and Ted had squared them for life with a bottle of whisky and a tin of corned beef. 'It was me who told him to do it,' Sophie said. 'You've always got to square your neighbours. So I don't see how anybody can give him away.'

Ivy noticed a grimace from her brother, who would be the last to like what was going on. Nor could Leonard see any sense in it. Ted had given his oath and, willing or not, should do his duty with the rest of his pals, though when he said so they laughed and told him to do something which he would rather not. Such people couldn't be altered by words, and the more in the wrong they were the less you could expect them to be. Some can change, and others can't, and the world has to depend on those who can. Having tried his best with both Sophie and Ted, he had got nowhere, finding an obstinacy in Ted that, when he could forget to dislike him, called for pity.

To shelter him and put up with Sophie was a test that would probably go on forever: he could not do other than endure, a familiar state which allowed him to maintain an aspect before the others of seeming not to, such supposed indifference being the only form of protection.

HEADLINES XXVIII

FIVE MILLION FOREIGN WORKERS IN GERMANY.

US BOMBERS RAID BERLIN.

COAL STOPPAGE IN NEW SOUTH WALES.

EIRE REJECTS US REQUEST THAT AXIS
REPRESENTATIVES BE REMOVED FROM EIRE.

FOURTEEN HUNDRED TONS OF BOMBS DROPPED ON
CASSINO MONASTERY.

WINGATE'S FORCES LAND IN REAR OF JAPANESE
LINES IN BURMA.

GERMAN TROOPS OCCUPY HUNGARY.

A THOUSAND RAF BOMBERS ATTACK FRANKFURT.

WINGATE KILLED IN PLANE CRASH.

CZERNOWITZ CAPTURED BY RED ARMY.

FORTY-ONE

A space under the stairs for hanging coats was a common archi-
tectural priest-hole in houses whose every cubic foot was needed
for storage. The kids had played there till it lost its glamour as a
place of concealment. Some people crouched in them during air
raid alerts as if they would be safer in the dark, or until gunfire and
bombs shook it sufficiently to indicate that they might not be.

Leonard spread a bucket of whitewash, cleaned off cobwebs and
set it up as a wardrobe. Back from work he noticed a cardboard
box behind two of Ted's suits and a coat of Sophie's: a dozen
bottles of White Horse whisky within, as well as stockings and
cartons of cigarettes. He laid them on the kitchen table. 'Did you
know about this?'

Paul was dressed in his cadet uniform, about to go to a parade.
'How could I?'

'I just wondered.'

'I knew some funny business was going on,' Ivy said, 'because
I often hear him coming in at five in the morning.'

'I seem the last person to know what's happening in the
house.'

'Haven't you noticed Norma?' She didn't care to worry him,
though thought it time he knew, not wanting him to wait till the
end of the war before kicking them out of the house. 'She's always
got proper stockings on.'

He turned from the fireplace, speaking softly as if someone
else might hear. 'I thought she pilfered them from work. Or she
stole something from there that she swopped with somebody who
worked at a stocking factory. I think half the town must live on
bartering what they thieve. At least since I met certain people.'

'It's about time somebody told the police where he is,' Paul said,
putting books into a haversack.

'Don't you dare,' Leonard said. 'Keep your mouth shut.'

'He's a deserter, ain't he? And he goes out thieving every night.'

'Even so, it's nothing to do with you. Stay out of it.'

Paul's face was pale, hand shaking as he gave his hair one last comb at the mirror and adjusted his cap – fearful at having argued with his father. When he had gone Ivy leaned forward to hold Leonard's hand. 'You've got to leave her, Dad.'

'It's easier said than done.' He sighed. 'But don't talk to me about that. I know my own mind on the subject.' He wished to God he did. Or even that he didn't, knowing only that Sophie was living with him and they were together for better or worse. After four years getting used to her ways it would be a waste of his suffering to leave her now, though he couldn't doubt it would be better if he did. He could only tolerate her in bed by telling himself he was fucking a prostitute he had found on the street and persuaded to come home for the night, so that it didn't matter who she was, and he could even enjoy it, or at least not want to get the pot from under the bed and vomit. The residue of loathing for himself wasn't as bad as the bare hatred he felt for Sophie and her betrayals. Any mechanism which allowed him to hold back the imperfect world was valid, though he reached for a newspaper to clear such rumination from his mind.

Ted came in wearing a suit, collar and tie, suggesting he hadn't been at work on any building site.

'Are these things yours?'

He made a bad job of a smile. 'I'm looking after them for a mate of mine. He's shifting digs and don't want anybody to swipe 'em. It's only for a day or two.'

Leonard stood before the mantelpiece. 'Get rid of it.'

He turned to Ivy. 'Any chance of a cup o' tea, duck?'

'I mean now.'

He was startled at the menacing tone. 'It's like that, is it?'

'I want 'em out. This minute.'

'I can't.'

'You can, and you will.'

'They've got to stay. You see, Leonard, I'm in a bit of a fix. Don't let me down. It's only for a couple of days.'

'I'm not having stolen goods in my house.'

'They aren't stolen. What do you take me for?'

'You bloody idiot. Get 'em out of the house.'

Ted faced him with a smile. 'It ain't your house, and you know it.'

True enough, but he had forgotten. It didn't seem important. For some reason he couldn't now fathom they had taken the place in Sophie's name. God knew what tale she had spun to the agents, but it explained why she had been so set on them leaving the old one. He had thought it didn't matter, wanted to please her, and she said the rent would be her contribution to the housekeeping, fair being fair. 'I don't care whose place it is. If the police walk in and find this stuff we'll all be for the high jump. So I want it out – this minute.'

'I won't, I tell you.'

'Oh, yes, you will.'

It wasn't much of a laugh he mustered. 'We'll see about that.'

'I'm running this house, no matter who's got the rent book.' Leonard unlooped his jacket. 'The Guildhall's close enough.' He knotted a scarf and tucked it in against the chill evening. 'I can't have you taken in as a deserter, I'm too soft, and that's your business, but I'm not going to have stolen goods in the house.'

'You'd shop me, would you?'

Leonard pushed him into the chair when he stood before him. 'I expect there's a sergeant on duty at the desk.'

Ted wasn't sure enough to start a fight. 'That's the sort you are, is it?'

'Make up your own mind about that. I'll be back in half an hour.' Ivy wondered why he couldn't act in such a decisive way with Sophie. So did he, but then, what she had done, and was doubtless doing, was only a crime against herself.

Ted wavered, a hint of tears. 'You don't need to go for the coppers.' He scooped the things into a corner of the table. 'It's nearly dark, so I can take it to somebody who'll buy it.'

Leonard was at the back door. 'You should have thought of that already.'

'I'm getting shut of it, look.' Ted pulled at his arm in the yard. 'I am, I am.'

A few birds flittered over the smoking chimneypots looking

169

for worms or crumbs in the tiny plots of back garden. Some hope they had. He didn't care whether the neighbours heard or not. 'It's too late. I'm not having such things in my house ever again.'

The gate clattered, and Sophie came towards them between lines of washing. 'What's all this about? I can hear you a bleddy mile off.'

'He's off to the Guildhall, to shop me.'

'I found his hoard of stuff under the stairs.'

She pushed them along, glad no one was out in the twilight to hear. 'Shut your stupid gob, and let's get back inside.'

Leonard broke free. 'I'm still going.'

'You coppers' nark,' Ted shouted.

Sophie groaned. 'Pack it in, the pair of you. And get rid of it,' she railed at Ted. 'For Christ's sake' – closing the back door after them. 'I've been worried about it for weeks.'

Leonard wasn't surprised that she knew.

'What could I do?'

Red faced but silent, Ted took his parcels away.

'I hope he'll be all right,' she said.

'He will be.'

'He might get stopped in the street. They look at anybody carrying big packets these days.'

'They didn't stop him when he carried it in here,' Leonard said, 'though I expect it was darker then.'

She stared into the fireplace, thinking how she had always wanted to find someone who was as perfect as it was possible to imagine. This she had known to be most unlikely, but apart from Leonard's jealousy, which at one time upset her because it put her off enjoying what she couldn't help but do, she sometimes thought him as close as she could get to that kind of man. 'So you would have shopped my son?'

He had no answer, unwilling to be interrogated.

'I'm getting to know what you're like at last.'

She wasn't, and never would. These days he hardly knew himself what he was like, until he did something that brought such a remark from her, then at least he had one opinion to confirm or deny. 'Let's forget it, and have some supper.'

She stood. 'I'm not staying in with somebody like you. I only came back to get something from my handbag.'

To plead would be useless. You won and lost at the same time, but it was the loss that was felt most sharply. The banging of the door shattered the ice around his heart, and he tried not to let Ivy see his tears.

HEADLINES XXIX

RUSSIAN TROOPS ENTER ROUMANIA.

FLEET AIR ARM LEAVE *TIRPITZ* CRIPPLED.

GOEBBELS IS MADE SOLE ADMINISTRATOR OF BERLIN.

RED ARMY REACHES CZECH FRONTIER.

SWEDEN REDUCES EXPORT OF BALL BEARINGS TO
GERMANY.

ODESSA CAPTURED.

GENERAL VATUTIN KILLED.

UK DEFENCE REGULATIONS PROVIDE DRASTIC
POWERS FOR INCITING TO STRIKE.

ALL TRAFFIC STOPPED ON DANUBE DUE TO MINES.

JAPANESE OFFENSIVE IN INDIA FAILS.

HOME OFFICE BANS ALL OVERSEAS TRAVEL.

FORTY-TWO

'Dear Sam, I don't know where you are, these days, but I hope it isn't too bad and that this gets to you and finds you the same as it leaves me. Everything is going on all right here, and there is nothing to complain about, though I suppose it would be all the same if there was. The Russians are bashing the Germans so we all hope the war will be over soon, though it has already been on longer than the last lot, which if you remember is what I always told you would happen, so God alone really knows when it will be over.

'Ivy has come out of the sanatorium, as I've already told you, and she is now getting much better sooner than I could ever have hoped for. She goes out for a good walk every day come shine or blow and looks all the better for it. We always have a long talk about you in the evening. Even Sophie asks about how you are now and again. I show Ivy your letters, and she shows me the ones you send her.

'Paul is getting on very well in the Civil Defence cadets, and also at work, where he's still in the packing department. He's a good lad, and likes everything but doesn't say very much. He's out all the time with his pals, so we don't see much of him. He's never got a spare moment, which is the same for all of us, and just how it should be. Everyone's got to do their bit, no doubt about that.

'Eunice is a sergeant now and hopes to be going abroad. I expect you'll have heard from her about that yourself. It will be another worry for me if she does go, but I suppose I should be glad because she will. She's been wanting it for years. As long as she stays with the pals she's made she'll be in clover.

'I'm getting on all right at work. There's more than plenty to do because we've got to keep the trains rolling. Nottingham's the same old place. I expect you'll recognise it when you get back, to which event, as if I need say it, we are all looking forward. A lot of grumbling goes on but when didn't it?

They wouldn't work hard if they didn't grumble, some of them anyway.

'Well, this is a long letter, but I do sometimes have an hour on my hands. I just wanted to let you know how things are. Look after yourself. Your loving Father.'

HEADLINES XXX

RAF BOMBERS DROP THIRTY-SEVEN THOUSAND
TONS OF BOMBS.

CONFERENCE OF COMMONWEALTH PRIME MINISTERS
OPENS IN LONDON.

JAPANESE LOSE HILL 551 IN ARAKAN.

SQUADRON OF MOSQUITO BOMBERS DESTROY SINGLE
HOUSE AT THE HAGUE.

GANDHI FREED ON MEDICAL GROUNDS.

FORTY-THREE

Midweek, but why had Ted changed into his suit? Now she knew:
'Let me take you to the pictures, duck. It'll do you good to get out
once in a while.'

His hair was Brylcreemed, face washed into a florid self-
confidence. But the smell of sweat still came through.

She had walked around the town, along Castle Boulevard and
into the Park of big houses and trees, marvelling at the pale green
buds on their bending twigs, the sun warming her face. A soldier
on guard at an army office had whistled after her. 'I've been out
already.'

He laughed. 'Don't you like Robert Taylor?'

'I don't know him.'

'Me, I fancy Rosalind Russell. I wouldn't mind coming across
her one o' these nights.'

She didn't think he was likely to.

'It's a shame, then. I'd give her what-for.'

Leonard was on the nightshift, and as for Sophie, maybe you
could say the same for her. 'I dare say you would.'

He leaned forward. 'Still, you ought to let me take you to the
pictures at least.' Cigarette smoke drifted across. 'I work hard,
and don't get much spare time.'

She was surprised to hear there was any such thing. 'Well,
nobody does, do they?'

'I earn good money, any road up.'

'Do you?' A while had gone by since she had seen him in
overalls. 'I didn't think you'd done much clocking-on these last
weeks.'

He scoffed. 'Hark at who's talking. All you do is knit.'

She dropped a stitch, caught it up, and went on with the long
pair of socks. 'I occupy myself.'

'Who are they for?'

'My Dad.'

'I thought he'd got plenty already.'

Had he been looking into the cupboards to find out? She wouldn't put it past him. 'They're for next winter.'

'We might all be dead by then.'

She knew that wan and babyish smile, and wondered how he could go on living if he thought like that. 'I don't imagine I shall be.'

He laughed at her ability to be certain about the future. 'Nobody can tell, can they?' then fell silent for a few minutes to savour the gloom he had caused.

'A lot of soldiers might be dead, and that's a fact.' Sam could use the socks and mufflers, because if he was in hot places now he would need woolly things for when he got back.

He was hypnotised by the movement of her fingers. 'More fool them.'

She said no more, not about that, anyway, because it was nothing to do with her. Even if he hadn't been a deserter she wouldn't have gone to the pictures with him. She liked being on her own in the parlour. These days it was warm in the evenings and she didn't need a fire. But he had followed her in, not realising that he wasn't her sort, though exactly what her sort might turn out to be, well, she didn't know, either. How could she? Anyway, it wasn't Robert Taylor, think what he liked.

'Come and see Cary Grant, then.' He had found a way into her thoughts. 'I've got plenty of money' – he jingled some – 'paper money, as well. If you don't want to go to the pictures, let's have a night in the pub.'

'Oh, leave me alone' – sorry she had snapped, but he was getting on her nerves with the same old boring song.

His face looked as if it had been dipped in scalding water. He smoothed his hair by the mirror, and fastened his jacket. 'You stuck-up bitch. I only wanted to take you somewhere nice.'

The slammed door shook the plant on the table, as if that too had been frightened by his fierce look. Good riddance to bad rubbish. She shouldn't have said that, either, fingers trembling as she continued with her knitting.

HEADLINES XXXI

COMMANDER IN CHIEF OF THE JAPANESE FLEET KILLED.

BRITISH OFFENSIVE IN KOHIMA.

RUSSIAN FORCES CAPTURE SEVASTOPOL.

US BOMBERS ATTACK BERLIN.

FORTY-FOUR

On her way back from getting the week's rations Sophie saw two tall Redcaps in raincapes at the end of the street and went in to warn Ted. Ted wasn't in. Well, he wouldn't be, would he? She supposed it was just as well, because then they would have spotted him on his way out. Norma was toasting her knees at the fire: 'He left ten minutes ago.'

Cobblestones shone in the rain, and cold wind sent water lacing across the slates and between the chimneypots. The Redcaps walked to the main road and on towards the river. Sophie put on her coat, glad Leonard wasn't in to see her alarm. 'We've got to go and look for him.'

'I'll get wet,' Norma said. 'I hate getting wet.'

Sophie pulled her upright. 'You'll get my fist if you don't shift. I wonder why they're looking for him now, after all this time?'

'Perhaps he's been shopped. I know somebody as would be glad to do it.'

'You want your brains testing.'

'Stop it, you're breaking my arm.'

Sophie didn't know how to find him. Two people couldn't be everywhere. But you had to try, because if he was caught you would never forgive yourself, and he'd blame you forever. Still, you might just bump into the silly bogger whistling along the street as if he hadn't got a care in the world. Kids – they didn't know they were born, these days.

Leonard sat reading *The Daily Herald*, glad Sophie hadn't gone out, but too tired to wonder why, or care much if she decided to. The clock chimed eight, supper dishes clattered in the scullery, and he must have dozed, for suddenly it was nine. Norma was ironing a blouse with an electric iron, which Ted must have brought in. Leonard imagined the house from which it had been purloined, one of the posher sort up Mapperley, which would also have a

179

sewing machine, a radiogram, refrigerator and vacuum cleaner. The motorcar would be under a tarpaulin sheet because they couldn't get petrol. There was a market for anything these days, since only items for the war effort were manufactured. Norma wore a wristwatch bought, so she said, from someone at work.

Ted came in with a suitcase, like a man back from travelling, heavy duty trench coat dripping rain. At Leonard's glance he said: 'Don't worry, Mam. It's empty. I wouldn't bring a dead pig into this poxetten place. Somebody might shop me.' He wouldn't speak directly to Leonard, believing you must always be on your guard with narks in the offing.

'Hang your mac in the scullery.' An odour of toasting bread filled the room. 'We had a couple of Redcaps nosing around the street this afternoon,' Sophie said.

The man of the world, with his recently grown moustache, was suddenly one of the hunted. 'Where, how and when?' he demanded in a single breath, then over again while eating what might be his last meal on earth. 'Are you sure? Are you dead sure?'

'You think I can't tell a Redcap when I see one?'

Leonard didn't know why, but found something to smile at. 'They might have been looking for another chap. Redcaps aren't so rare, these days.' It seemed reasonable to think so, and didn't matter to him one way or the other, but no one thought he was being helpful. The anxiety in the room was like that before going over the top. Ted in danger threw clothes into his suitcase. 'They won't get me.'

'Where shall you go?'

'I'll drop you a line, Mam.'

'Have you got any money?'

'A bob or two.'

'Just a minute. They aren't at the door yet.' She took her handbag from the shelf, and pushed notes into his hand.

He thanked her. 'So long, Mam.' There was no word for Leonard, who had none for him, either. 'If I end up in clink send me a cake with a file in it.' The door slammed, but then he was back, mackintosh belted, trilby soberly on.

'The bad penny,' Sophie said. 'What now?'

He left his case by the door. 'I forgot to say so-long to Ivy.'

She was glad he was forced to go, but wished him luck.

Sophie felt unloved because nobody loved her children. She felt too forlorn to go out. They might be a rough lot, but they had done no one any harm as far as *she* knew. 'You might have said goodbye to him at least.'

'Yes, I should have. I'm sorry.' He hadn't felt so at the time. She sat at the table, staring before her, no interest in a book, or the wireless, only alive when with people whose talk amused her. 'I'm worried about him, all on his own. Where will he go?'

'He'll be all right.'

'Do you think so?'

He stroked her wrist. 'I promise. Whether I like him or not is neither here nor there, but I do know something about him.'

'I'd hate to be on my own like that.'

'Well, you're not, so stop worrying.'

A week later she received a letter from a Mr James Thompson, at the Acme Hotel in Glasgow: 'Just to let you know where I am, and don't call me anything but yours sincerely, or they'll have my guts for garters, because that's the name I go under these days. I bought a new identity card from a tattoo artist.'

Leonard was surprised at such neat handwriting on the single sheet of blue paper. Some school had taken trouble over him, and that was a fact. 'Aren't you going to send a word or two back?'

'I expect he's somewhere else already. Once he's on the run there'll be no finding him.'

He remembered her tears on the evening he left. 'I'm sure he'll be waiting to hear.'

'Do you think so?'

'A kid of mine would.'

'I suppose you're right.'

'I'm sure I am.'

'Is there any writing paper?'

When he fetched some from the table in the parlour she sat looking at it. 'I'm not very good at writing.'

He wondered whether she was any scholar at all. 'I'll do it, then, if you like.'

'No, I can manage.' She wrote a few sentences, speedily and

with no trouble, then sealed the envelope. 'You can do the address, though.'

Was it so important that she was afraid of getting it wrong? Or did she want him to have a share in the work? He wondered what Ted would think on seeing he obviously had. 'I suppose you want a stamp now?' He always kept one or two behind the clock.

'I don't know what I'd do without you,' she said.

By the pillar box on the main road, he felt tenderly towards her. The light was draining out of the sky, glowing yellow on dark houses. She needed something from him that no other man could give.

He looked at the King's head on the stamp, tempted to tear the letter up. Such a son was unworthy of her, but he let the letter drop.

HEADLINES XXXII

US SENATE EXTENDS LEND-LEASE UNTIL JUNE 1945.

JAPANESE LAUNCH OFFENSIVE IN MANIPUR HILLS.

JAPANESE CUT PEIP'ING-HANKOW RAILWAY BY
CAPTURE OF LUSHAN.

MR CHURCHILL GIVES ACCOUNT OF BRITISH AID TO
RUSSIA.

FORTY-FIVE

He had never seen Eunice looking so smart, so *complete* in herself, but then, she always had been. And she had taken her standards of dress, whenever she had needed to, from girls in the office, then from the woman she lived with, and latterly no doubt from the drill sergeant. She had put on weight, shining buttons pushed out in front, making the stripes on her tunic as plain as if she had been born with them. 'We might be going overseas. Egypt, or Palestine. You never know.'

She sat on the chair, to let him have the sofa. Young old-maidish Muriel had gone shopping, a nice excuse to leave them alone. 'If you do, I'm sure you'll look after yourself.'

'You can bet on that.' She refused his offer of a cigarette. 'Muriel goes mad at fag smoke, and I was never keen on it. I've got some good mates in the army, though. We take care of each other.'

'That's how it should be.'

'There are six of us secretaries, and our work is very hush-hush.'

'So I won't ask anything. I know all about that from the last lot. But I'm more than happy to see you're getting on.'

She put the cat down to avoid hairs on her skirt. 'It's because I work hard.'

'You've always done that.'

'We've got to do our bit, and I don't mind. In fact I like it better than I've ever liked anything.' She spoke with a softness in her eyes as if such sentiments might need tears for them to be properly believed. 'It's really got me out of the old life. I can't wait to get overseas.'

'You might even bump into Sam.' He saw a newsreel on Pathé Gazette: palm trees along a road, army lorries going both ways, Eunice in one and Sam in the other, time to wave and shout the name of their camps before each was lost in a billow of gritty sand. Or she walked along a quayside, white houses packed on a hill. A gun-bristling launch tied up in the harbour, and Marines jumped ashore. Sam would spot her first . . .

'Wouldn't it be marvellous?'

He nodded. 'It's happened before. One of my friends in the last war heard somebody shout out when he was wounded further up the trench. He said he would know that voice anywhere, and ran to find that the man was his brother. He hadn't even known he had joined up! Both of them came out all right, as well. They were chaps from Leicester.'

'I'd love to go to Palestine' – his story had no relevance – 'and see all the places they showed us on the magic lantern in Sunday School.'

'I'd envy you, if you did.' Solid in her expectations, he could only marvel that she had turned out so well, when so many had not, or would not, or maybe could not.

She picked up his thoughts. 'How's Sophie and her kids, these days?'

He had been dreading such an enquiry, which he knew would have to be dealt with. 'Very much as usual' – surely not a lie.

'Ivy told me a bit about the dance she leads you.'

Then why did you ask?

She had little of her accent left, which made her judgements seem more condemning. 'I can't say it sounds as if they are doing their bit, and that's a fact.'

'I'm always hoping they'll improve.' He knew she was right, but tried to bring a smile into the matter.

'You're too optimistic, Dad. You always were. It stops you doing anything. I'm sure they'll never improve.'

'I suppose not.'

'It's in their blood. I'm glad to find Ivy looking so much better, though.'

'It's a miracle,' he said. 'The best thing that's ever happened. I can barely understand it.'

'She had good treatment in that sanatorium.'

'Perhaps God looked after her.'

'Well, it was better than if she had stayed at home.'

'I suppose so.'

'I know so.'

'Me and Sophie took care of her as best we could. You just weren't there to see it.'

'*She* never cared for anybody except herself.'

He wouldn't chide her for being censorious, though maybe it would do her good if he did. But it wouldn't. She couldn't change, and not only because she was young. Being his daughter must have more than enough to do with it. He and Sophie had been together over four years and he couldn't make it come to an end. He decided every morning to do so, but each day drew him on with its ordinary routine, and for hours together he forgot his yearning for a different life. By evening he was back in the familiar state of apathetic exhaustion that put all things beyond consideration.

He tried to correct her without starting a quarrel, since she might be away for years. 'You're wrong. Sophie's a good-hearted woman. I've got no reason to complain.'

Her mouth was firm so as not to counter his barefaced untruths, and he disliked the fact that it took such an effort. He reached for her hand, and knew that if he had been young, and she had not been his daughter, she was the sort of woman with whom he might have gone through life. 'Don't worry about me, duck.'

'Oh, I'm sure you'll be all right in the end.' She smiled at last, and touched his arm, then drew her hand away too quickly.

He added what he knew to be unnecessary, yet hoped she might appreciate. 'Just look after yourself, and come home safe for me and the family.'

Muriel walked in and he knew it was time to go. Her old flatmate looked miserable at the coming separation, and he couldn't blame her for that, though it made him smile as he said goodbye to Eunice.

FORTY-SIX

Ted stepped into the house as if it was his and nobody else's. He had no luggage, and wore overalls under a sports jacket. Working his way into a meal of bread, cheese and piccalilli, his tone was halfway between bravado and fear. 'I had to run for my bleddy life.'

Paul turned the pages of his first aid book, and pretended not to be listening.

'It was all right at first, because I got myself a job putting up some barracks. But yesterday when I was coming back to my digs I saw the coppers going into the house. I chiked with other people on the street, and could see they was in my room, so I knew they must have found what they was after. That Bible-backed old landlady must have snitched. They couldn't see me for dust. I got a lift on a lorry as far as Carlisle, but still had a quid or two in my pocket, so I took a train from there.'

Sophie was glad Leonard wasn't in, and Paul was too busy with himself to hear much, though Ivy would tune her ears up from the parlour. 'Do you think the police will come looking for you?'

'Of course not. They'll be *calling all cars* for a bloke named Jim Thompson, the silly prats.' He stripped to the waist and washed in the scullery, changed into the one suit he hadn't taken with him.

'I see you're back, then,' Leonard said, in from work.

'You'd need glasses if you didn't.'

'Scotland was too hot to hold him,' Paul said.

'What's it got to do with you?'

'Not much, I suppose.'

'Did you get your mother's letter?' Leonard asked.

'Letter? What letter?'

He took torch, sandwich-tin and notebook out of his haversack. 'I posted it, that I do know.'

Ted laughed at the idea of a letter from Sophie. 'The last one

I had from her was when I was in a Remand Home, and the bleeders who ran the place took the money out that she put in it. They spent it on themselves.'

'Maybe she forgot to post it. Or put the wrong address on the envelope.'

'Nar – she sent it all right. She swore to it afterwards. And she never lies, not to me anyway. Maybe the postman nicked it.'

'Nobody interferes with the Royal Mail. It'd be Dartmoor at least, if they did.'

He laughed again. 'Where was you born, Leonard? In Dreamland, or what?'

'You wasn't born.' Paul looked up. 'And that's a fact. You was hatched.'

'Shurrup, nipper.'

'Shut up yourself.'

'Stop it, you two.' Leonard opened the pantry door to see if anything had been left for supper. 'Sophie's gone out, then?'

'Does it bother you, Leonard?'

'Not any more.'

'She hopped it, ten minutes before you came in.'

He ate slowly. A hot dinner in the canteen during the day didn't call for much in the evening which, he thought, was just as well.

Ted, in the excitement of his escape from Scotland, wanted something to be angry about. 'I hope you aren't thinking of shopping me any more.'

'I don't have it on my mind at the moment. Anyway, I've never shopped anybody in my life. I haven't had occasion to so far.'

'You was going to once.'

Leonard poured tea for the three of them. 'As long as you don't bring any stuff you've nicked into the house you'll be as safe as you can expect to be anywhere' – a promise which Paul didn't agree with at all.

HEADLINES XXXIII

COMMITTEE SET UP TO ADVISE UK GOVERNMENT ON
WORKS OF ART STOLEN BY THE ENEMY.

FIFTH AND EIGHTH ARMIES ATTACK GUSTAV
LINE IN ITALY.

A HUNDRED CARRIERBORNE AIRCRAFT
ATTACK SURABAYA.

CASSINO MONASTERY TAKEN BY POLISH TROOPS.

FORTY-SEVEN ROYAL AIR FORCE OFFICERS
SHOT BY GERMANS.

FIVE THOUSAND ALLIED AIRCRAFT ATTACK AIRFIELDS
AND RAILWAYS IN FRANCE AND BELGIUM.

BRITISH AND US FORCES LAND AT ANZIO.

THIRTY-SEVEN THOUSAND TONS OF BOMBS DROPPED
ON GERMANY AND GERMAN OCCUPIED TERRITORY.

FORTY-SEVEN

Ted was so little at home that Ivy wondered if he hadn't rented another place. She couldn't think why he stayed, wished he would leave altogether, but he came now and again for a meal, and maybe to borrow money from Sophie who rarely looked happy at seeing him, knowing she would never get it back. The number of suits in his room allowed him to dress again with the care and style that resembled his father's – if indeed he was Charlie's son.

When Ivy was alone he would ask her to go out with him. Sometimes he'd come with a box of chocolates, but after he left she would set them on the kitchen table for the others.

Leonard was on days, and Sophie out somewhere, so he made himself easy in the best chair and said: 'I only want to talk.'

'I can't stop you.'

'Well, not only that. I wouldn't be much of a man if I only wanted a bit of jaw-jaw, would I? Do you know why I came back from Glasgow?'

'How should I?'

He caught her interest, as sensitive as a fox to the wind. 'The coppers weren't after me at all.'

She believed nothing he said.

'Folks tek owt in. I just got fed up because I was on my own and missing you, duck. I couldn't turn a corner without seeing your lovely face coming towards me. The trouble was, it always passed me by. I'd chase after a woman on the street, and when I tapped her on the shoulder, thinking it was my lucky day, she turned around with a face like the back of a tram-smash and told me to scram.' He smiled, and went on: 'Even when I was out at night and up to no good I kept seeing you. "What's our Ivy doing here in Scotland?" I thought. But it was always somebody else. I love you though, you know that, don't you?'

They were words she had always wanted to hear, but not from him. 'I don't know what you mean.'

'Of course you do. But you're too stuck-up to listen.'

Whenever she thought he would come for a visit she got up and went for a long walk, using him to make herself more healthy so that one day she would be able to go out and get a job. But she couldn't be absent all the time. 'I suppose that's the way I am.'

'There's nowt wrong with me. Is there?'

Some girls could find him goodlooking, but she knew too much of the bad side to be interested. 'Did I say there was, then?'

'I know I'm not the sort of young chap a person like you might like, but still . . .'

For a moment his sad aspect made her worry. 'I don't know you, do I?'

'I can't help being different. And anyway, nobody's perfect, are they?'

'Who's talking about that?'

He no longer stared at her face, but turned to the window. 'When I was eleven I got sent away to a Remand Home because I nicked a few bars of chocolate. Mam didn't much care. Or she couldn't, I don't know what. In court before they took me off all she said was: "Well, I'm sure they're going to feed you well where you're going." Not that Dad cared, either. Both of 'em's always had too much on their plates to worry about me. But they pasted me something rotten at that Home. They was devils to us. I daren't tell anybody what they did. You don't know one half of what goes on in the world.'

He had put up with a lot, and she shuddered at the horrors he found impossible to tell about, but whatever they were he didn't have to desert from the army and thieve for a living, did he? 'I dare say I don't.'

'If I get caught it's the glasshouse for six months, everything at the double. Our big packs will be loaded with stones. They kick you half to death if you don't look sharp. I'll only go back to that lot if they drag me there. It's their war, not mine. But I don't know why I'm telling you all this. I suppose it's because I love you. So why can't you love me back? Anyway, I'm only asking to take you to the pictures.'

She stood up to walk out of the room, pitied him but couldn't like him. He put on a look that would tempt anyone to trust him, to love him even, making it easy to imagine how many women he had taken down.

But not her. She pushed him away, wanted to love but felt none for him. His strong arms crushed her, but she kept her eyes open, at the same time avoiding his white-blue glare, hoping she wouldn't have a haemorrhage if she pushed him with all her strength.

Breathless, he let her go. 'Christ, you'd think I'd got three eyes and a hare lip.'

The icy brush had painted her face white. She stood clear. 'Get going.'

The scullery door banged, and Paul called: 'Is anybody in?' – home from a stint at the Civil Defence.

'A kiss wouldn't hurt you – just one.'

'I've got a right to be left alone.'

He moaned with offended pride. 'Bogger you, then. I know where I can get all I want.'

Paul drew the curtain aside, hat in hand to see what was the matter. 'Is he bothering you?'

'No.' Ted pushed his way out. 'She was bleddy asking for it, though, I'll tell you that.'

She laughed at her brother in his navy-blue uniform, whistle, lanyard and shining boots, fresh-faced at sixteen, and knowing enough of the world's ways from his work in a warehouse. He had grown so quickly that his trousers were slightly short.

'I just don't want to talk to him, that's all.'

'I don't blame you,' he said, 'I hate his guts.'

HEADLINES XXXIV

FIFTH ARMY ENTERS ROME.

ONE THOUSAND GLIDERS AND AIRCRAFT LAND
TROOPS BEHIND GERMAN DEFENCES IN NORMANDY.
THIRTEEN HUNDRED BOMBER COMMAND AIRCRAFT
HIT TEN COASTAL BATTERIES. TOTAL NUMBER OF
SORTIES INVOLVE THIRTY THOUSAND AIRMEN.

US TROOPS CUT RAILWAY TO CHERBOURG.

RUSSIANS OPEN OFFENSIVE ON KARELIAN ISTHMUS.

NORMANDY BEACH HEAD FIFTY MILES LONG.

FLYING BOMBS LAND IN SOUTHERN ENGLAND.

FIRST SUPERFORTRESS RAID ON JAPAN.

ARMS FACTORY IN COPENHAGEN DESTROYED
BY SABOTEURS.

RUSSIANS WIPE OUT FIVE GERMAN DIVISIONS
NEAR VITEBSK.

RAF DROPS FIFTY-SIX THOUSAND TONS OF BOMBS IN
SUPPORT OF INVASION ARMIES.

FORTY-EIGHT

Maps in the atlas-gazetteer weren't of a good enough scale for following the war, and too many pages had gone missing, so Leonard bought a Map of All Fronts for a shilling, and pencilled the to-ing and fro-ing on that. Spread out on the few occasions when the table was cleared, such grids and colours created an awesome diagram of death and ruination in whichever direction you looked. He heard the news on the wireless, and brought home the *Herald* or the *Mirror* now and again, noting the stepward closing in of forces against Germany and Japan. Because of caring little what Sophie got up to he took more interest in the war, though the daily progress was so slow it looked set to go on forever.

Firewatching, and overtime at work, meant little opportunity for mulling on either, but if he put in too many hours, so did most other people as well. You either had too little or too much, the nature of life being that nothing was ever just right. Few needed encouragement to soldier on in such a cause, which was as well, he told himself, at the sight of two heavy drayhorses pulling a brewers' wagon up the incline of the bridge. At least the Second Front had started, more than indicated by the constant rumbling of engines above thin cloud.

Sophie went out every evening, and rarely came in until morning. If he was on days he wasn't there to tell her what he thought, which seemed best for them both. But he came home one day to find a telegram on the table concerning his son – and that, he muttered, was the last bloody straw. Since Sam's enlistment he had dreaded the worst, could only say thank God he was wounded, and hope it was no more than a 'blighty' one, but further enquired to himself what exactly wounded in action might mean, as the paper shivered between oily fingers. Was Sam blinded? Had he lost an arm? Or a leg? Was it in any case serious enough for him to die? And in what part of the world was he? For a Marine it could be in sun or snow, among mountains or on the sea, and no matter where Leonard searched on his map of every front he ended up puzzled, but glad all the same that he had looked.

Red Cross trains from France came daily through the shunting yards, khaki-painted enclosed carriages whose red insignia called only for pity. The wounded were brought home *soonest possible*, as the phrase had it, light cases kept near the front, then sent back into action. If Sam's condition was serious he could be shipped home, so maybe in a month a letter would come from a hospital close enough for him to be visited. Then again, he might hobble in without warning: 'Hello, Dad! It was a bit rough out there, but I'm all right, as you can see!'

The features of Sam's face that Leonard recalled would be nothing like what he wore now, and that was a fact. He knew himself willing to die for the privilege of exchanging the hurt of his son. At the front in the last war no worry about his parents had entered his mind – no more, he supposed, than Sam thought of him, though maybe he does now, with time to himself. He glanced from his stupor at Sophie's pale face under the headscarf.

'I hope the telegram wasn't bad news,' she said.

'Bad enough.'

'I left it on the table where you would see it.'

Reports on the wireless at least suggested that the war might be moving at last. Time never stood still, things continually changing, bad times passing more slowly than the good, but change they also must, even if only because the world turns on its axis twenty-four hours a day, and goes around the sun once a year. 'Why didn't you open it?'

'I was frightened, duck.'

Would Sam, when he left the Marines, be able to find a job, get married and have children, like those who came back unscathed? 'We've got no secrets, God knows. You could have come to work and told me, then.'

'I suppose so.' She leaned close, and he thought how strange it was that from the pit of his desolation she seemed more goodlooking. 'What does it say?'

'He's been wounded.'

The clock ticked their lives away, ticked everybody's away,

ticked out Sam's as well. No one escaped. Destroy every clock, but the click of every clock had its purpose and you couldn't live without them, weren't permitted to, they measured the goings out and the comings in, calculated every farthing of the hour's labour, the opening and closing of doors, all actions and births and deaths.

'I thought it was worse,' she said. 'That's why I was frightened of opening it.'

'It's bad enough.'

'I wanted you to do it on your own, duck.'

If he found her hard to understand it must be a hundred times more difficult for her to understand him, so in fact how could it be possible for her to understand herself? Such revelations came because he had suffered at living with her, and though the suffering had diminished after he had accepted her for what she was he suddenly felt less able to live with her, since the suffering she caused which made it feasible was now overridden by anguish for someone else.

He recalled holding Sam's warm hand on a visit to the marshalling yards as a boy. Arthur White had taken him out for an hour on a shunting engine, delivering him back with a glow in his eyes that lasted for days.

'Don't cry, love.' But he was too far gone to cry. If he was crying – and perhaps he was, because why not? – it was for Beryl, who wasn't here so that they could comfort each other over the plight of their son.

Nevertheless, it was Sophie who, saturated with his grief till it became more than she could bear, turned to him for comfort.

HEADLINES XXXV

MINSK RECAPTURED.

CARRIER-BASED AIRCRAFT ATTACK IWO JIMA.

BRITISH AND CANADIAN ASSAULT ON CAEN.

VILNA TAKEN.

GANDHI SAYS: THE WORLD HAS MOVED ON.

ATTEMPT TO KILL HITLER FAILS.

RUSSIANS CAPTURE MAIDENEK
CONCENTRATION CAMP.

FORTY-NINE

She would never be ill again, and that was all there was to it. Nobody could make her, if she didn't want to be. Death had come once, but she cut off his foot when he put it in the door. Even if Death tried the same dirty trick again, and succeeded in killing her, she would still have had the pleasure of thinking she would live forever.

Everything flowed from a determination to feel yourself beyond the damage that illness could do, saying that if any *person* tried to harm her there was her brother Sam, a knight in his Royal Marines uniform, striding into street or field, or even stalking the darkest part of the forest to protect her.

But Sam was no longer able to, because his leg had been blown off in a minefield, and he was a cripple. She wasn't invisible any more. Crying would do no good: she had done enough for a lifetime, though would have done more if it would help. Crying put a veil over the eyes that stopped you seeing what was really going on, and had never done anybody much good.

She switched the light off by the door and hurried back to her warm patch in bed, the only part of the house she was happy at that moment to own. Sitting with Sam on the attic floor after opening their stockings at Christmas, the smell of Jaffa oranges had been heavy in the cold air. He showed her how to arrange the box of coloured bricks to make words, happy as a teacher, patient when she was clumsy.

Back from Malta he would find his father living with a woman like Sophie Waterall. Ivy imagined him making Leonard see sense, clearing Sophie with all her tribe and chattels out of the house. But no, he would hobble in with his crutches and a false leg, and that lot would laugh in his face.

'Move up, duck,' he said. 'I thought I'd just come and keep you company for a bit – if you don't mind.'

Ted had decided that she wanted him but didn't realise it, or she wasn't able to ask. She needed a man like him to go all the way without permission, so that by the end she would know she had longed for him all the time but hadn't been able to say so. Some girls didn't know their own minds, especially the sort who couldn't say what they wanted at any old time, and didn't have a clue how to ask for it.

The door hadn't rattled, and bare feet made no sound as he came in and pulled back the clothes, cold air touching her flesh. Silence and stealth were second cousins to his strength, but from sideways on she sprang and struck at his face, spitting for him to get off. The night was too black for shadows, better if she didn't see him. He pressed at the shoulders but her feet were free. Strength coming back from she couldn't say where, she hit at his eyes, screams as silent as the dark was light. Her fingernails scythed him and she felt his blood on her.

'You bag!' He jumped away. Paul hadn't come home, often stayed at his duties till midnight or later, drinking tea and talking with the wardens. Why, oh, why? Oh, what was he up to?

She lifted herself from the floor, craving to yet not putting on the light as he maybe hoped she would, afraid of the dark now. 'Get away.' She moved towards the table. 'If you come near me again I'll blind you.' Speaking gave her courage, but speech was a shining light to him, therefore she would keep silent. In her hurry she pulled out the wrong needle, threads of the long scarf zig-zagging. Both needles were of the best steel, and she held them before her, the table behind, his awful words no more than one would expect: 'That's all I want.'

She didn't need Sam to rescue her, he was within her, and she was a long way inside herself because she had his courage.

There was beer and she didn't know what else on his breath. 'Just let me love you.' He had no clothes on, and she felt his touch. 'I shan't hurt you, my darling' – such words far worse than his swearing.

Their breathing blocked her ears, a sea scraping the shore. If she didn't speak she would be sick, tears wetting her face, but she would stay safe and not let him do it.

'Come on, duck, let's finish what we've started.'

He had begun nothing. She supposed he could see in the dark, strange that enough of his strength passed to her for her to stab straight at his hard muscle. 'Needles of the finest Sheffield steel,' her father had said when he bought them.

He screamed at the burning points, not even the booze making them painless. Why she said it she would never know, but the words spoke themselves. 'I've got a knife.'

He believed her, frightened of the demon she had become: not the child's play of a man with fists, but of a woman he knew nothing about. Being used to the dark from his nocturnal thieving he might even laugh, yet couldn't know what the folds of her nightgown hid, or guess each move before she thought of it herself. A lateral switch of her arm, sensed but not seen, made him run for the door.

If she pushed the table across he would hear it as a challenge, so she stood, waiting, couldn't rely so much on her instinct now that he was out of the room, not sure he wasn't just outside, or standing by his own door across the landing.

Had he gone into his room, pulled bedclothes over him and fallen asleep? If he'd done so she should have heard it, and even recalling the minutes made it impossible to say yes or no. She had been alert, so should have known, but didn't remember, which made her tired and wish for day or death but knowing that neither could help her yet.

Any noise of defence might bring him back, the scrape of table legs on lino a sound she didn't want to make because the only course was to keep silent. In any case to move furniture might bring on a relapse.

Matches and a candle lay by her bed for emergencies, and she filed the needle against the box to calm herself, slowly to make no noise, down and again down, as if sharpening a pencil with a knife in the kitchen.

He closed his door but she couldn't say which side he was on, knowing his cat-like tricks even before they reached his own brain. Maybe he was already half asleep, musing no harm done, and he would greet her in the morning: 'What was all that fuss about last night, then?'

But if he was prowling she would sit him out because it was no longer safe not to in such a house, and she wouldn't sleep till she was calm, if ever that state returned in her life. The room was blind, a night that, no matter how you stared, showed nothing. She hated having known anyone as she had him, in those moments, someone she least wanted to be close to but who had got into her to that extent at least, so that for the time being she couldn't like herself and wanted to scream with rage.

He listened at the door, she knew it, measured out her breath in the smallest amounts. The hairspring of his balance to action was unmoving. A sense of danger thickened the air. She wanted to shout for help and bring everyone in the street to the house, but didn't, couldn't, feeling as ashamed for what had happened as if it had been her fault.

He walked away, impossible to say whether or not he would burst back in, so she scraped and filed at the knitting needles till the emery strip along the box was worn away and she wished she had another.

FIFTY

In winter you walked to work in darkness and came back in darkness. The streets were always the same, a smell of frost and freezing mildew. To sleep away the few hours of day was no delight, because the noise was at its height. But the dreams came and went, though they seemed barely natural.

Now it was July and though less careworn his worry in the shunting yards still persisted till he got home at seven in the morning. There were no air raids and he knew of no reason for anxiety, but these days he never wanted to leave the house. Everyone had to take their turn of duty at this round-the-clock regime, and worry in any case was like breathing, an inseparable part of his being.

A man on a milkfloat rattled his bottles, calling out to him: 'Hey up, mate!'

People were cheerful in the morning, full of hope for the new day, or at least of joy that another had been put behind them without too much bother. An early-lit fire in every house set coal fumes piercing the throat, little different from train smoke breathed in all night. The milkman looked hard at Leonard. 'Don't you know me, then?'

Was it someone he had been at school with, met in the Trenches, known once upon a time at work? He wore a tie and pin, and no doubt a jacket under his green overall, smart for a roundsman. 'Know you?'

The thrust-forward features turned hyena-ish at his puzzlement. 'You ought to, though we only met once, in The Rose of England. And I'm never mistaken in a case like that.'

Leonard remembered.

'Still leading you a dance, is she?'

The Ministry of Labour had nailed him into honest work at last, total war that had come a bit late in the day for such as Charlie. 'I'm in a hurry.'

A man on his doorstep wearing Monday-morning dungarees waved a hand: 'It's today I've got to be at work, not tomorrow.'

'Take your bleddy sweat.' Charlie glared at having been robbed of an altercation with Leonard. 'It's coming.'

He would do a different route so as not to bump into him again. Nightshift or not, Charlie or no Charlie, he was glad to be walking towards the one and only refuge, to make the usual fire and sit with a mug of tea, mulling mindlessly through his bread-and-jam breakfast.

He took off his boots, making no noise on the stairs in case Sophie slept, though he doubted she was in because her best coat had gone from the hook downstairs. A packet of twenty Players was kept in reserve behind the washhandstand, and he put them in his jacket before going down to relish his first fag of the day in solitude.

A creak from the ceiling told him Ivy was awake. She was often early, after the sanatorium routine. He would say hello, let her know he was in the house, though she had probably heard him, in spite of his stealthy opening of the back door.

A rhythmical whisper came through the thin wood when he tapped. 'Go away. Go away.'

'It's only me, duck.'

She valued her privacy, he knew, like any young woman. Her tone was sepulchral, spoken by the stomach rather than the throat, which chilled his heart. 'Go away.'

She stood by the window, sleeves halfway up, a knitting needle in each hand. 'Whatever's the matter?'

Her face was bruised, hair swept by a wind that made the room too bleak for her. 'I thought you was him coming back.'

What had happened, in the world they were unlucky enough to live in, came to life before he could know what it was, in the feeling of dread that dominated all his senses. 'Who?'

She hugged the bedclothes, as he shut the door and pulled down the window.

'Him,' she said.

'Did you fall down?'

'No. It was *him*, I tell you.'

He sat on the bed. 'You've got to tell me, duck.'

'It wasn't a dream.'

'How do you mean?'

'He wanted to force me. He came in.' She couldn't say his name.

'Was Sophie in?'

She moved her head, the stare fixed, a glitter of madness.

'Where's Paul?'

'I don't know.'

'Who was it, then?'

'That Ted.'

The idea finally broke anchor. 'Did he do anything?'

'No.'

'You can tell me.'

She opened her eyes, a shake of the head more circular than positive. 'He couldn't. I would know, wouldn't I? I didn't let him.'

His muscles hardened. 'Has he gone out?'

She wanted something to happen, life being at an end if they lived any longer in this house. 'He went to his room. But thank God you've come back, Dad. I can't tell you how long I've waited.'

He opened then closed her door as if a gnat wouldn't stir at the movement. All the same, if he didn't hear her crying his heart would break. She had a lot to cry for. What else would bring her back to the surface of her life?

He stepped across the landing thinking he would go down to the kitchen for the butcher's knife, which someone like Ted had grown up to die by. The stairs spoke, despite his care. He stopped to listen. Slaughter him. Slaughter him. Even the drawer was hard to get open, cutlery rattling when it leapt forward.

At Ted's door he kept the handle from springing back and waking him. Everything depended on silence. Socks, braces, shirts, picture magazines and fag packets untidied the floor, a half curtain across the window. He was into and out of the blankets, a hand behind his head in perfect sleep. Leonard's heart went like a drum at how the guilty could look so innocent.

He rehearsed the deed, sweat running from his face. Accustomed to living as two people he let the animal half control his actions.

The palm chafed, telling him either to wield the knife, or let go. His hand shook from holding it too tightly to use, impossible to grip harder. He would be hanged for murder, no quarter given. He was not yet cunning enough to have lost his reason. Since Ted had not managed to force her, you couldn't kill an innocent man. If he had forced her he would certainly have murdered him.

His hand still craved to but, shackled by the Commandment, his foot stopped at a half-filled tea mug, a spoon leaning from the yellow circle. Ted would sleep till ten if no one disturbed him. Making sure Ivy's door was closed, Leonard went downstairs to put his boots back on.

FIFTY-ONE

People on the streets weren't dolls, they were real, and you were one of them. No one could point at you for any misdemeanour: you were free to walk where you liked, to get on a bus for work or play – or not, as the case may be. The war was being fought so that you could choose to live by the rule of law.

A barge pulled under the bridge by a horse showed that animals worked for their daily bread. Dogs guarded houses, cats stalked and destroyed rats to keep the city clean. Every one thing was on earth for a purpose, and labour made the world tolerable for yourself and others. Ted did not fit into the scheme of live and let live.

He had intended walking a straight line from house to Guildhall, but he crossed Canal Street and turned up by the Castle walls. On the top parapet where he had taken Beryl the air was clear and you were nearer the sky. A good day showed you woods and fields. You could also send your body bouncing a hundred and fifty feet down till the spirit died with it, and when all those had died who could remember you, you were forgotten, and might never have lived. But lighting a cigarette calmed him and, in the meantime, having done his nightly stint, he had another job to do.

Between two uptilted handcarts he went into the café near the newspaper offices, fourpence on the counter for a mug of tea. Drowsy from steam and food smells he forced his eyes open. Sometimes on nights he seemed not to have slept for weeks. 'There's a young man at home called Ted Waterall. He's a deserter, and you might see things in the house that have been stolen,' he would say to the sergeant at the desk. His tea cooled, and the serving woman squinted as if wondering whether he had a home to go to. He downed the next one quick enough to scorch his tripes.

Two police cars took the corner from the back of the Guildhall and turned by the Mechanics Institute into Parliament Street. A couple of Specials went up the steps, and he followed, to do a bad turn for someone who deserved it more than most. But sending him down would be a favour, the making of such as him, though he might come out worse than he went in. However he reasoned, he would nark on someone not fit to be loose in the world, and to get his own back because he had tried to rape his daughter.

He turned from the vestibule and walked down the steps. Narking wasn't the word if a man was guilty, but he still couldn't do it. He would get to jail in his own good time, whether or not you gave him a push.

Sophie called him, and he walked to her across the street. They stood on the pavement. 'I thought you was at home having your breakfast,' she said.

And if she had been in bed Ted might have behaved himself.

She no longer bothered to hide anything. 'I was at The Flying Horse.'

There were still men wealthy enough to take her out. 'Oh, yes?'

'He gave me ten quid.'

More than a week's wages. 'You must have a fair bit in that tin box by now.'

She held his arm. 'I haven't counted it lately.'

He wondered what people would think to see a railwayman just off his shift walking down the street with such a woman so early in the morning. When they got back he was going to pull Ted out of bed, punch him all the way down the stairs, then go back up and throw his belongings into the street. And if she wanted to follow he would give her some assistance as well. 'It's going to be a nice day, at any rate.'

She found it strange that what she got up to didn't bother him any more, as if there had been some kind of safety in their wild arguments and his unhappiness. Such quiet endurance was hardly to be trusted. 'What was you doing at the police station, then?'

A bread van had collided with a car coming out of a side street, and bus traffic queued to get by. He wanted to kill her with silence. Or he was sulking again. She lost all patience with him. 'I thought I asked you a question.'

'I wasn't doing anything I shouldn't have been.'

'I didn't think you was.' She stopped by the canal bridge. 'It was a very funny place to see you, though.'

He could hardly have said the same about her. 'I had business to attend to.'

She supposed he had, otherwise he wouldn't have been there, would he?

'I know, but I changed my mind when I got inside.'

'And why was that?'

He wanted all talk to be finished. 'How should I know?'

'You must know.' She snapped her hand free, pulled him to a halt when he started walking away. 'A chap like you don't go into a police station for nothing.'

He wouldn't argue on the street. 'I'll tell you about it when we get home.'

'I want to know now.'

Her manner hardened him further, and he did not care whether she followed, though she would because his home was still her lair and, like it or not, there was damn-all he could do about it till they got there.

The street was straight and flat, a thoroughfare with houses close to on either side. A squad car was slanted across the far end, with two Redcaps watching. People leaned from windows or stood in doorways. 'What's going on, then?' Sophie said to an elderly policeman.

'We're making an arrest at number twenty-one. You'd better hold back a bit. The silly young bogger must think he's going to be hanged, the fuss he's kicking up. We'll have him down in a bit, though. We've dealt with harder cases in our time.'

She pushed by. Men in overalls and women wearing snoods and jackets were passing on their way to work. 'It's at my house. I live there.'

Leonard made up a nightmare that left him standing in cold dread across the street, of how Ted had woken and gone back into Ivy's room while he, Leonard, had been shilly-shallying about town unable to make up his mind whether or not to turn him in. And this time he had forced himself on her, or perhaps done worse, till her screams had alarmed the street.

A policeman wearing glasses pushed Sophie away from her door.

'Leave him alone,' she shouted, at Ted's roar as they prised him down the stairs. 'You rotten bullies.'

Fully dressed, white-faced, going nowhere, Ivy from an upper window smiled. 'Stay calm,' Leonard called. High clouds blew themselves along. It was going to be hot, and they would be at the seaside first, though a dog barked as if wanting to follow them. A woman with two kids in a pram pushed a way through, and the police took a hard look at a bundle of washing balanced on the handles as if it might be stolen goods.

'The bleddy rotters,' Sophie screamed. 'I know what you're like. Leave him alone. He's my son.'

A flash of navy-blue uniform across an entryway caught Leonard's eye, haversack at an angle telling him who it was. Paul's face was Jack-o'-Lantern pale, but a smile wasn't far off. Leonard fixed him by the arm. 'Where have you been all night, you useless bogger?'

'On duty,' he said. 'Where do you think?'

'Was it you?'

'I don't know what you're talking about.'

A ginger-haired bantam of a man, a mashcan swinging, told the policeman he was off to work: 'There are too many bleddy thieves around here,' he added, pausing as if he would be glad to offer him a light. 'It's about time somebody took him away.'

'We'll pull you in as well if you don't shut your mouth,' the policeman said, as if he hadn't yet had his breakfast.

Arms and legs fastening into any groove, shirt torn and shoe off, Ted's words ricochetted through all backyards: 'He narked on me! Leonard snitched. He towd 'em everything.'

'Whoever did saved us a lot of homework,' the policeman smiled.

'I'll get you, though,' Ted called, 'poncing off Mam for all those years! Selling my stuff on the black market as well. He always said he'd shop me, Mam. I'll tell 'em he tried to kill you as well. It was attempted murder!'

At a signal from the sergeant the car drove close, and Ted got in as quietly as if it were a taxi. Leonard, pale at his tirade, could have sworn there was a grin on his face.

HEADLINES XXXVI

BRUSSELS LIBERATED.

US AND FRENCH TROOPS ENTER LYONS.

BLACKOUT RESTRICTIONS RELAXED IN BRITAIN.

FIRST V2 LANDS IN LONDON.

WARSAW APPEALS FOR HELP.

US FIRST ARMY CROSSES GERMAN FRONTIER.

POLISH GOVERNMENT THANKS RAF
FOR AIDING WARSAW.

FRENCH FLEET ENTERS TOULON.

RATIONING OF TEA AND COFFEE ENDS IN CANADA.

US HEAVY BOMBERS DROP SUPPLIES TO WARSAW.

JEWISH BRIGADE GROUP TO TAKE PART IN ACTIVE
OPERATIONS.

FIFTY-TWO

'*Now* I know why you was at the Guildhall,' she cried, still thinking that after a good row all would be as before. But he handcarted as many of his goods out of the house as possible in one band of daylight. Norma labelled him with the same curses used by Ted, and worse, and the neighbours had better value than a seat at the Empire, inclining him to believe that the tribulations of *The Chocolate Soldier* were bland by comparison.

'You went crawling on your belly to the coppers, to get your own back on all of us. You gave my son away, and didn't expect to see me as you was coming down the steps, did you? I'm finished with you, then. I'll hate your guts forever. And *don't* take that out of the house, you graballing swine. It's mine. Charlie gave it to me.'

Charlie hadn't: a marble-topped table Beryl had sat at during her last months – when she was able – to put on powder and rouge, and brush her thinning hair. Declining a tug-of-war, he walked out of the room, but in half an hour he was back, and when she blocked his track towards taking it he did what instinct ordered.

She fell, a hand at her stung face.

'I only want what's mine,' he said, ice-cold at what he had done.

Lips moved, but she couldn't talk. In any case, he had heard it all before. She would never change, so what could you do with someone like that? He thought tears were to be her final eloquence, until she said: 'Nobody looks after people like me except myself. Nobody can.'

'You wouldn't appreciate it if they did. I loved you, you know I did.'

'No, you didn't, or you would love me now.' Useless to say more. She wiped her cheeks. 'Get going, then. I don't want you. I don't need you.' You couldn't be comforted for the loss of your son by the one who had betrayed him. Then again, Ted was as daft as his father, who had been in and out of prison for as long as she had known him. He was still her son, though, and belonged to her. As always, she spoke without thinking, but that was the only way she knew to change her life. 'Go on, move. I don't want to see you any more.'

And that was that.

HEADLINES XXXVII

RUSSIANS ENTER HUNGARY.

SAN MARINO DECLARES WAR ON GERMANY.

CANADIANS BEGIN ALL-OUT ASSAULT ON CALAIS.

AIRBORNE TROOPS WITHDRAWN FROM ARNHEM.

EIGHTH ARMY CROSSES RUBICON IN
ADRIATIC SECTOR.

EISENHOWER TELLS GERMANS THE ALLIES COME AS
CONQUERORS BUT NOT OPPRESSORS.

FIFTY-THREE

When in his own house and in thrall to Sophie he had barely known who he was, but now that he was mere flotsam in a place that belonged to somebody else he had never been more solidly himself. 'It'll only be till I can find somewhere to go,' he said to Albert and Gwen one day after work. Sam was in a hospital near Portsmouth, and would be home any day now, he wrote, so it's not worth your coming to visit me.

'I'll look for a house in Radford,' Leonard said. 'I expect that'll be far enough away, though it'll be a fair hop from work.'

Albert lent him a bucket of coal, so he sat by the fireplace after Paul and Ivy had gone to the pictures. They shared one room, but he had never seen them so happy. He was back among people who had pot dogs on the parlour shelf, brass shellcases by the front door to hold umbrellas, pictures and photographs on the wall, a plant on the sideboard, curtains at the windows and between the rooms, the house permeated with a homely aroma of pumice, vinegar and perhaps tobacco.

Neither Albert nor Gwen seemed plagued by the kind of brute tension that strangled thoughts at birth. If they had their savage moments he couldn't imagine when they let fly. And if they were sometimes unhappy then he didn't know what unhappiness was, unless it didn't exist, or was called by another name.

'You're well shut of that lot,' Albert said. 'Of course, I twigged she was your missis, and I'd seen her a time or two in Yates's, but I couldn't mention it. It were none of my business.'

True enough, and Albert would not have told him anything he hadn't known, as Albert no doubt realised. 'I miss her, though.'

'You're bound to.' Gwen was a tall thin woman with grey hair and glasses. 'People miss a bad 'un a lot more than they miss a good 'un, though I could never think why.'

He couldn't imagine Sophie felt the lack of him, but if she did come knocking at the door and asked to live with him again he wasn't sure that he would refuse. Recalling her was a torment he could do without, but at every street corner on his way to work he hoped to see her coming towards him with the same smile and promising embrace that had induced him after only the second meeting to ask her into his house.

He went through the next months half asleep all day because he had been half asleep during the night from thinking of her with tenderness and blind loathing following in such rhythm that he thought he would go mad, while holding firm enough not to miss any of his shifts.

He found a house to let from where he could walk across the River Leen and into the fields before breakfast. The sound of church bells on Sunday took him so far back that he knew it was not the area in which he would meet her. Standing between the hedge and tender heads of wheat glistening with dew, he recalled the music of those same church bells as a boy. At that time he hardly knew what they were, and felt that everything was wonderful in the world. Such a paradise was never to be reclaimed, but at least he had the good fortune to remember it.

When he read in *The Evening Post* that Ted Waterall had asked the magistrates to take thirty-two other cases of thievery into consideration, Leonard assumed that the police had helped with a bit of rough stuff when it came to details.

The sweet grass he walked through brought Sophie to mind nonetheless, and he had to fight himself away from haunting those places where he might see her. Unable to go back to such madness made him feel like an old man, though he hoped he was not.

HEADLINES XXXVIII

US FORCES INVADE OKINAWA.

ALLIED TANKS HUNDRED MILES BEYOND THE RHINE.

YUGOSLAVS CAPTURE SARAJEVO.

PRESIDENT ROOSEVELT DIES.

VIENNA LIBERATED BY RED ARMY.

BELSEN CONCENTRATION CAMP REACHED.

THE GRAND DUCHESS ARRIVES
BACK IN LUXEMBOURG.

NUREMBURG CAPTURED.

FIFTY-FOUR

Sam got down from the train with kitbag and case, ruminating that the new leg stiffening could be as much due to a rheumatic ache as war's catastrophe – as far as anybody knew. Or it might have been caused by an indisposition after cricket: a ball overarmed by a big strong fool of a teacher had once collided with his kneecap and made him limp for days. They could think what they liked, especially the doddering porter who looked sicker than the old woman whose gear he was pushing on a barrow. 'Here comes the Prodigal, Dad!'

Ivy, less adept at hiding her tears than Leonard, thought he looked neat in a navy-blue pinstriped demob suit, trilby and white shirt, with grey-and-blue tie.

'Cheer up, duck!' he said, a softened accent but the same homely words as he kissed her. 'I wouldn't have known you if you hadn't been with Dad. Everything'll be all right now I'm home, though.' His hand rested firm but damp in Leonard's, then he went back into the carriage and came out twirling his stick. 'They know I won't fall down, but they insisted. Can you imagine, a hundred per cent pension at twenty-three!'

Leonard saw the black hair of Sam's mother flattened against a sweating forehead when he lifted his hat, dark eyes embedded in as thin a face as if he had been through days of fever, a curve to his lips that hadn't been there before.

The air was fresh beyond the station, Sam was glad to note, though life had always been worth living whether the air was clean or not – as long as you had all your senses sharp and morale second to none.

A bus conductor on the pavement demolishing a choc-ice waved at an acquaintance going by, and Leonard saw the man's whole life in that greeting, as if there had been no trouble (though he knew better) thinking that his own life might have been similar, if he hadn't been himself. Yet it was only by being born to what he had become that made his happiness so intense on welcoming his son, and he envied no man by the roadside. You can never be anyone except who you are, and as you get older you become even more what you always were.

Sam buttoned his mackintosh against the wind. 'It's nice to see the old town again.' His nostrils analysed the nostalgic layer cake of smells: glue from Bitterlings by the river, diesel fumes from buses, train smoke and chimney grits, and even a cut of fresh breeze when it got an edge in. 'It's all very familiar.'

'You must have been in some rum places.' The weight of Sam's kitbag made Leonard feel young again, despite being just as anxious about him now that he was home.

'A lot. And one of them – well, I'll never want to see it again, will I?' He looked straight before him, at the comings and goings of the station across the road while they waited for a bus. 'A soldier takes his secrets to the grave, Dad, as you always said. But I'll tell you where I caught my packet when we get home, if you've still got that old atlas we used to look at together.'

'It fell to pieces.' Ivy recalled the enthusiastic destruction of the pages by Sophie's kids, as if any sign of other parts of the world was a threat to them.

Leonard felt an icy area at his left temple as if the skin, being made of paper, would let the cold go in and extinguish his brain. A funny sensation, till he rubbed it away. 'It was out of date. We'll buy another.'

The mannerism was new to Sam. 'It would have been even more useless now the war's finished.'

'You think it is?' In the bus they sat close to the platform. 'Under that Hitler they'll go on fighting till there's not one brick left standing on another.'

'You're wrong. It's all but done. Then we'll do those people in the Far East. Haven't you opened a paper lately?'

Even so, it was hard to believe the end was close. All who had eyes could see what evil was. Not that there'd ever been any excuse, but who would imagine such horrors the papers showed? Grisly stacks of corpses, and prisoners at the barbed wire perishing from hunger. 'They'll go on fighting in the mountains. They've done too much wickedness to give in easily.'

Sitting by the fire at the day's end Sam wanted to know: 'How's the war been for you, then, Dad, while I've been away?'

'We kept the home fires burning.'

'I know you did. But you had a few bombs, didn't you?'

'Only one real raid.'

Sam tapped the bars of the fire with the poker. 'I heard about you and that woman Sophie.'

'Did you, then?'

'Well, you told me. And Eunice dropped me a line or two. She didn't like her all that much.'

'We make mistakes sometimes.' And still do, Leonard might have added, as if everything with Sophie had happened yesterday – no, even in the last five minutes. Now that he thought of it, never once had she said she was sorry, even if she hadn't meant it, nothing to lessen his torment. She didn't have the imagination to think it necessary, or perhaps she had been too frightened to say anything in case an ensuing quarrel turned so bad he threw her out. Maybe she supposed that saying you were sorry didn't stop there but led to serious talk, and she wasn't confident in that kind of world. 'I liked her, and won't deny it.'

Sam drummed the table, as if he couldn't manage without sound. 'I wouldn't have minded what you told me. I never thought you were made of stone.' They sat by the diminishing fire. 'But you ought to get married again.'

He laughed, to hide his surprise. 'Me? What a daft notion.'

'There has to be a few widows knocking around.'

The war must have stopped him growing up, whatever he had gone through, though Leonard couldn't doubt he would soon recover lost ground. 'I haven't seen any.'

A shade of pre-soldier humour passed over his face as he lit a thin cigar from a box he had brought home. 'Plenty of women, in fact, especially in a place like Nottingham.'

To talk about Sam's own prospects would surely be more interesting. 'If it's a case of "every old sock finding an old shoe" I suppose I could get in the queue, though it probably stretches from Slab Square to Derby by now.'

'You never sign off, Dad, that's all I know. You're only fifty, aren't you?' He got up, not too steady after a long day. 'I'll just hobble to the pub and bring back a quart of ale. Will you share it with me?'

'I will, but let me fetch it.'

'We'll go together. I need a bit of air. I get sick of being inside. I must get my life organised. There's a Civil Service exam I'm going to study for. If I pass I can get a good job. It's a career I'm after now. The war was only an interlude, and time waits for no man, especially if he's only got the use of one leg.'

Leonard made a move to help, but Sam eased him away and stood by the door. 'We was on a Greek island, and knew that if the Germans captured any of us we'd be shot. I'll never know how my mates got me back after I trod on that mine. But they did. I'm resurrected, Dad. Do you remember when I used to talk about exploring the world? There are no more dreams, and that gives me a lot of strength.'

Leonard gripped his son's shoulder, tears running down both their cheeks.

HEADLINES XXXIX

61,000 CIVILIANS KILLED AND 86,000 INJURED IN AIR
RAIDS SINCE THE BEGINNING OF THE WAR.

POLES TAKE BOLOGNA.

RUSSIANS ADVANCE ON BERLIN.

US FORCES LIBERATE DACHAU CONCENTRATION
CAMP.

MUSSOLINI SHOT.

HITLER COMMITS SUICIDE.

FIFTY-FIVE

Ivy saw herself cycling along country lanes, on a high ladies' bike with a case guarding the chain and mudguards to stop her frock getting splashed, even puffing up a hill to look into a magical valley of farms and cottages beyond, as if all her dreams were there, and would one day turn real around her. Sometimes a friend, shadowy and unobtrusive, would be by her side.

Sam clubbed in a couple of quid, Leonard made up the rest, and Paul forked out a pound so that she could have a lamp and pump on a secondhand boneshaker. Paul also saved up his coupons to buy her a box of Black Magic.

She had money of her own since starting work in the office of a factory making jerseys and cardigans, but they told her to keep it in the savings bank, because she would be twenty-one today and might need it for other things soon. They had talked the complot over late one night.

Bus tickets and dust gusted up from the river, the kind of wind that made people lively while doing their Saturday shopping. Leonard was looking forward to a game of housey-housey in the railway club with Sam – a proud man with his wounded soldier-son – whom they had left at home reading and resting his leg.

Turning a corner, Ted came towards them, and Ivy by instinct aimed her walk to one side hoping he'd go by. 'It's that Sophie's lad.'

The name was mangled by a passing trackless, but Leonard's heart still beat so heavily he thought he would faint. Ted stopped in their path, beret at an angle, two modest ribbons above the battledress pocket, boots glowing below his gaiters. 'Look who it ain't, then! How are you all?'

'Very well,' Leonard said. 'As you can see.'

'I'm off for a sup of ale before dinnertime. You've got to keep the old belly tanked up, eh, Leonard? I'll buy you a jar as well, if you like. After all, we had some rum times together, didn't we?'

Leonard had to admit that he was right.

'I'm sorry I shouted all that about you when the coppers took me in.'

'What do you mean?' But he hadn't forgotten.

His tone changed, and there was something of an old man in the deadness of his eyes. People pushed around them on the pavement. 'Oh, I know it wasn't you who shopped me. I don't hold it against him, though.'

'Against who?' Leonard said.

He smiled. 'I didn't have to be Einstein to figure out it was your lad, did I?'

'We've got to let bygones be bygones,' Ivy said.

He was happy she spoke. 'I know, duck. That's what I tell myself all the time. I'm just back from Germany, and it was a bit rough over there in April, crossing that river – the Rhine, I think. A shell blew me back in the water, and I nearly got drowned. I felt like a Christmas tree with all that equipment on my back.'

'I thought you didn't fancy being in the army?'

He stamped his boots as if on ice. 'Not at one time, Leonard, but I love living rough and having a go at the Gerries. Riding with the guns is right up my street. It's only the bullshit I could never stand. None of us could. But there ain't much of that on active service. Maybe we'll be having a go at the Japs next. It'll be a change, crawling around in the jungle.' He wasn't quite the same person to Ivy, and looked happy that she was halfway interested. 'I'll bring you a wristwatch for when I see you next time, duck. I can find all I like. You can swap a few packets o' fags for one over there.'

She wanted a watch, but not the way he would get her one. 'Don't bother about it,' though trying to sound grateful. Leonard couldn't imagine him changing, except that he had turned into a soldier. The question was impossible to resist. 'How's your mother?'

'She's got a Yank now, an officer in the air force. I'm supposed to salute officers, but the Yanks don't bother so much about that sort of thing, at least he don't with me. He wants to take her to America, so she'll have to ditch Charlie first.'

'Perhaps she'd like it over there.'

'Pigs might fly. She's had a rotten life, though, except when she was with you, Leonard.'

He said he couldn't think so.

'Maybe even I'll settle down some day.' He winked at Ivy, who felt a warm flush at her face. 'Norma got married last week. She had to, the silly bitch. He's a swaddie in the Green Howards. I feel sorry for her, though, as well.'

'So do I,' Ivy said.

Leonard was about to say 'Give Sophie my love', but couldn't trust such a message with someone who might sully it in the transfer. He was also no longer sure he would love her till the end of his days, or want anyone to know if he did, and in any case his love might be safer if he didn't commit it in words to this windy street. 'Remember me to your mother.'

Ted adjusted his beret. 'She often talks about you. I must be going, though. The ale might run out. I'll see you again some time, unless I run off to America as well. After I'm demobbed.'

'We'll be sorry to lose you,' Leonard joked.

'Ah, well' – he forced out a smile – 'thousands wouldn't!'

Ivy felt it was like seeing a relation depart. His back was straight, and he had lost weight. She was surprised at noticing so much but, having hated him, could not dislike him now. 'Good luck,' she called, before he turned the corner, not knowing what feelings came top in the scheme of her world, as if having died and been born again gave her the right to wonder.

HEADLINES XL

BERLIN SURRENDERS TO RUSSIAN ARMIES.

ALL GERMAN TROOPS IN ITALY SURRENDER.

RANGOON CAPTURED.

MR DE VALERA CALLS ON THE GERMAN MINISTER IN
DUBLIN TO OFFER CONDOLENCES ON
THE DEATH OF HITLER.

STREET FIGHTING IN PRAGUE.

GERMAN ARMIES SURRENDER IN HOLLAND.

UNCONDITIONAL SURRENDER OF GERMANY TO
WESTERN ALLIES AND RUSSIA.

VE-DAY. MR CHURCHILL BROADCASTS IN AFTERNOON
AND HIS MAJESTY THE KING AT NINE PM.

FIFTY-SIX

Sam thought his father was taking plenty of time dressing up to go to the club for a night out. But Leonard couldn't get the collar stud into the hole, hands at full stretch to behind his neck, vision looking directly on, a conundrum solved countless times with no previous bother.

After an unusual struggle the button slotted, by when his face in the scullery mirror was like that of a September tomato. He wasn't putting on weight, no thick neck to thwart. Next he ran a comb through his hair, and the quiff wouldn't stay put. He didn't need a haircut, but strands stuck out, a state he disliked. Corporation hair oil wetted his skull and livened him up because he was feeling dozy. His eyes wouldn't focus, brain full of liquid, and he was tempted to laugh but decided not to, rubbing his temples back into sense.

Not so much the skin of his face as his aching arms which fell away. No one would say there was anything wrong with me, he told himself, and neither would I; so get on with it, and live forever. He lifted both arms like wings to find that one was straighter, flexed them full out nonetheless, like the broken sails of a windmill trying to turn. He saw the picture of himself fighting to control his arms, till he decided he was fit enough to put on a tie.

Hitting the floor was a funny way to knock sense into himself, but he had no option, a point which, in that fragmented second, told him how options had never been open to human beings anyway, and that maybe those were better which took up the least time, and were beyond all dispute in their effect.

Pole-axed, was all he could say, taking a step backwards as if to save himself falling down a hundred flights of stairs, sleep promising to be priceless before it engulfed him.

HEADLINES XLI

KING LEOPOLD OF BELGIUM FREED BY US
SEVENTH ARMY.

FINAL ACT OF CAPITULATION RATIFIED IN BERLIN.

SOVIET-FINNISH TRADE AGREEMENT SIGNED.

RUSSIANS OCCUPY PRAGUE.

QUISLING ARRESTED IN NORWAY.

AMERICAN CASUALTIES IN EUROPEAN WAR NUMBER
ONE MILLION.

GERMAN GARRISON IN CRETE SURRENDERS.

NEW US ATTACK IN OKINAWA.

FIFTY-SEVEN

All power, straight to their heads, a trio of snake trails illuminated the round tower of the hospital, and the dome of the Council House. Peace would be more difficult than a war in which you'd had only to do as you were told. Sam had given himself the nod on that since his father's illness. Responsible for himself and others, he had to make decisions, and there wouldn't be so many orders which were more daft the less you could dispute them.

Leonard, a man of the old world that ought to be well and truly done with, stood nearby with two sticks to prop him up, one side of his face trying to come back from the dead, though it never would. He hoped the display of rockets and bangers would be the last explosions in his lifetime.

Ivy held her father's hand on one side and Sam's on the other. Both were warm. Or they were holding hers. It was hard to tell after a while. Leonard pushed Sam's hand away to indicate he was all right. Have it your own way. Paul couldn't tolerate his father's helplessness, so put on his cadet uniform to roister in the Market Square with his mates, hingeing his neck with the crowd to see what he could of the spectacle unloosed from Castle Hill.

Tree-trunks stored in the goods sheds had kept their smell, wood surviving the saw's teeth, the crash into undergrowth, and transport across the ocean. After storage and the cuts of ever-busy bandsaws they made planks from which people could view the Great Victory Benefit Show.

Fireworks had been manufactured for when hostilities ended, specialists, ex-Home Guards and soldiers on leave setting up the show in the Castle Ground to honour everyone's stint for the good of humanity during five long years and eight months.

Varying decibels of noise, reminding Ivy of guns and bombs mixing their wartime clamour, brought a relaxing joyousness from the crowd she was part of, though she couldn't think why her anxiety wouldn't go away, and wondered why everybody else didn't feel the same.

Miniature compartments of fuse and powder, pre-planned and ignited to the second, produced glamorous illuminations, Sam saying aloud but to himself: 'You can have it. I've seen enough, and what a shame Eunice isn't here to agree on the waste it all is. Or would she?' A letter to her commanding officer asking for compassionate leave might bring her back to see her father before . . . Before what? Well, the war had shown him that you had to die when the old gong sounded. In peace you could hear it long in advance, and had to be ready. No one lasted forever, love them though you might.

Lights spangled into a victory banner, then fell away to make room for a tapestry of Robin Hood in Lincoln green, hat tilted and bow arched, an arrow at the lurking sheriff or maybe even God Almighty Himself. They were getting it right at last and he let go Ivy's hand to take the stick from under his arm and rap it against wood, while the livid tableau, as perfect in its message as fireworks could make it, crumbled under cool air and gravity.

'Maybe that's the end.' Leonard tried to clap. 'I don't see what else they can do.' He slurred and blurred, an empty fury when no one understood. Ivy pressed his hand, an ear to his lips catching the wet, acting as if she had, which at least made him happy. Hoping he would one day wake up normal and not need their help at all, he had written with his left hand from the furthest insides of his damaged prison to make them bring him to the fireworks.

'I shan't forget tonight.' Trying not to cry would once have made her cough, a thought sufficient to stop her tears at Leonard's plight. 'Isn't it wonderful, though, Dad?'

Handclapping sounded like the city collapsing house by house, and out of the cheering a voice demanded to *see that last bit again*, which set them laughing. Such a comedian – a real card, no less! – relished how things were going, went on to demand *a full supporting programme*, the sort of person who put everybody at the picture house in uproar when the heroine near the end of a film was set for a course towards being *done-in* – strangled, blood-sucked, thrown by some madman of extra-human strength out of the castle window into a moat far below: 'Don't go, duck.

Keep away from that doorknob. Take no notice of him. Run the other way. Don't stare into the eyes of that picture on the wall' – someone who wanted the impossible, body and mind to turn from the track of doom which Fate had led them to.

History was coming to an end, or so it was thought, giving people eternity and longer to understand fully the evil done. Leonard's ruminations – slow as the slowest slow-motion shunting engine going from one extreme of the marshalling yards to the other, each point the corner of an eye and hardly ever to meet – were checked by streams of coloured light falling over sloping acres of slate, making him glad to be here.

Encouragement was mixed with jeering. Powder stank like hot dust and rusty iron, caught in his throat as the end of the rainbow sprayed good luck on to buildings in which people worked or lived, and a sunshade opened, from whose circumference streamed rivers of gold and red as if a wind blew among them.

Darkness made spots flicker before the eyes, till thunderflashes drummed the ground, diminuendoed by a fusillade of small-arms fire, and dulled by a clouding sky as if, like rain after Waterloo and all great battles, the night would end in a washout.

Leonard counted the moments through a two-minute silence which divided the performance, till each tick outran him, fight as he would, angry at Ivy wiping his cheek. 'Poor old Dad. You'll never be the same again.' But when this blooming war is over, no more soldiering for me – a world in which there was only the chocolate sort who carried no bullets. His watch swung on the chain, and Sam pushed it into his waistcoat pocket. 'Don't lose that, Dad' – or you won't know who you are any more.

Why is he so angry with me? Leonard wondered – old fool I've become.

Sam wished he hadn't brought him from the hospital, but Leonard got himself dressed, and would have gone into the street anyway. The doctor didn't advise it, he said, but beds were beds these days, and if he wanted to go out it might be for the best. He would have another stroke soon – though who could know for sure? But whatever happened he wouldn't last long. You didn't know what to believe.

A whistling quintet of rockets: work to be done. Leonard looked

230

up, couldn't remember a smile so wide. Dashing into the sky, they pinned out four corners and one stabbed into the centre, till a Union Jack was formed. Coloured lights drilled themselves, as if for the moment all would be well, and the multitude was silenced with hope for the future, as if every heart had stopped to encourage the design's success.

From the crowd came the same old nihilistic though uniquely local hee-haw. The Union Jack colours, played from the ground by their inventive puppet-master, for one static moment were halfway to triumph, but a few droplets of fire altered their ideas, as if in rebellion against doing the job like slaves or soldiers. Leonard worked out that no one, or anything, could be relied on to do their will. 'I want to go home.'

'You're tired, aren't you, my duck?' Ivy treated him like a schoolkid. 'Well, we'll go, then, if you like. I'll take you back and put you to bed.'

The colours disintegrated into all manner of bunting, which to Leonard looked like the slow melting of an atlas page, until the sky was so dark that no face could be distinguished from another, and the peace began.

HEADLINES XLII

DECENTRALIZATION OF GERMANY.

CHINESE TROOPS ADVANCE NORTH FROM FOOCHOW.

HIMMLER COMMITS SUICIDE.

BRITISH LANCASTER RETURNS FROM TRIP OVER
NORTH AND MAGNETIC POLES.

LORD HAW-HAW CAPTURED IN GERMANY.

FIFTY-EIGHT

The newspapers had it that Charlie Waterall waited one dark night on Trent Embankment, near the War Memorial. Who he was in the offing for no one was ever able to say, but all who knew him guessed it must have been a woman. The stubs of several cigarettes were strewn around, so he had stood there a fair while, and with some impatience.

A barely smoked cigarette that fell from his mouth when he was struck matched those still in his cigarette case, and because the case was in his pocket when a policeman found his body, as well as a lighter and several pound notes, nobody could say the reason for the attack had been money.

Behind him in the dark was the vast War Memorial, a lofty archway with colonnaded wings extending to left and right, with a balustrade along the front, and steps going down to join the flight descending to the river. The area was in darkness, but Trent Bridge, a few hundred yards to the left, was lit up now that peace had come back to the world. Some houses in Green Street and Frazer Road were also lit up not far behind. Perhaps Charlie's woman was expected from that direction, to meet him for a cuddle and something more after her husband had gone on the nightshift. Not knowing who the woman was, and who her husband might have been, made it more difficult to track the murderer.

Though not living with Charlie at the time, Sophie was called in to identify his body. Charlie's face and head had been smashed, it was surmised, by a large steel wrench, and only one side of him was handsome now, she thought. She also said to herself: good riddance to bad rubbish – words perhaps not so heartless because they prevented her fainting at the sight. As if to make up for such an unmarital reflection she wept hot tears at the funeral, and then went home to wait for her American who was coming on leave from Huntingdonshire.

HEADLINES XLIII

TOTAL CASUALTIES OF ARMED FORCES UP TO
FEBRUARY 1945 WERE 1,128,325 OF WHICH 307,210
WERE KILLED.

BRAZIL DECLARES WAR ON JAPAN.

GENERAL ELECTION. LABOUR LANDSLIDE.
MR CHURCHILL RESIGNS. HM THE KING SENDS
FOR MR ATTLEE.

ATOMIC BOMB DROPPED ON HIROSHIMA.

NAGASAKI BOMBED.

JAPAN SURRENDERS.

FIFTY-NINE

Paul got him to play draughts, but Leonard's brain was spent. Though Ivy fed him tea and slops, his collars no longer fitted. He was mostly in pyjamas, and they had set him up with a bed in the front room. One day Sam led him out for a walk but he fell down, a blow so fierce to the remains of his system that he couldn't get up again.

His last will was to struggle into and hope to finish Sophie's letter embedded in his heart, a letter she had never written but which he had forced himself to devise so as to go on living.

'Dear Leonard,' she could have said, 'it's goodbye now, and always was, even when we first met, because you shopped my son and only a mother is allowed to do that, and if she does, in any case, then God help her, because she shouldn't do it, either. I loved you only as much as I could afford to, but you ought to have believed I loved my son more – man and swine he can't help being and I'm sure will always be.

'I am myself, and gaffer of them all, of you and every man who I feel like loving even if only for a few minutes, because that is all all of them are fit for. You had more of me than any man, and you deserved it, and I hope you remember it, but I'm not sorry for you because at least you had me in your house a few years, and no man can be more privileged than that. I had you only when I wanted you, but you were lucky because all others who had me had to pay and only thought they had me in any case. They were the riff-raff of the world while you were special due to being by all accounts hard done by because I slept in your house. You often said it was my house and meant it, bless you, which is why I came as close to loving you as any man, and I will never forget that.

'I know you didn't really shop my son. You were too soft-hearted to betray anybody, but that was the reason I made up to leave you, and let you keep the self-respect that you deserved, your

235

generosity being untouched enough to keep you going in peace for the rest of your life.

'But I'm not out for peace because I know that since I was born that wasn't on the cards for me. No man can give me the sort of love a son feels in the comfort of his mother – knowing he will never be betrayed. I can never give that comfort to anyone except my sons, whose father isn't important because he is forgotten in the mixture of men I have known. I don't think any of my kids were Charlie's, which is one way a woman has of getting her own back on a man who doesn't know how to treat her. Charlie more than suspected this, and things got so bad I had to close forever even though we aren't in sight of each other any more.

'There was someone I loved before I came into the world, and once I got on it I knew I could never find whoever it was, which is true of every woman maybe. You were damned, though, as the lucky always are, in having known me, that's all I can say.

'Perhaps we should never have met, but we did, and you loved me as far as I was able to let you, and I loved you as far as I was able to let myself, though even so, we were never to meet like some people can because love had burned out of me before I was born – unless the fresh air did it when I was pulled from my mother. I could never be unhappy because I never expected love from any man to be perfect, so in that case I didn't try.

'PS I was sorry to hear about your stroke.'

SIXTY

Ted was a chargehand working for a building firm. In the thickening lime and wood dust while reconditioning a house he sanctioned a tea break for the men and drew a pile of browning newspapers from an old cupboard to sit on. He picked up one to read and in the deaths column saw: 'Leonard Graham Frankland passed away on 21 October, peacefully. Missed by Eunice, Ivy, Sam and Paul.'

'Well,' he said, with a faint shock of sadness, 'would you believe it? Poor old Leonard. I thought he had another twenty years.'

'Who's that, then?' said the mash-lad.

'Mind your own business, and get out of my way.' He folded the half sheet into his overall pocket, and posted it to Sophie who lived – so she had written – in a marvellous house in the country near Philadelphia, where she had everything she had ever wanted: washing machine, television, fridge and car. Herbert, her real estate husband, had a motorboat, and they went fishing on the nearest river. She had another daughter, and they would live happily ever after. She could never, she said, come back to England. All that was finished. The only man she thought of now and again was Leonard.

So Ted told *me* when I met him on the street five years after the war – convincing me, if ever I needed it, that Fate rules everything.

St Pargoire,
January 1991.

flamingo

Flamingo is a quality imprint publishing both fiction and non-fiction. Below are some recent titles.

Fiction
- ☐ The Naked and the Dead *Norman Mailer* £6.99
- ☐ The Kitchen God's Wife *Amy Tan* £5.99
- ☐ A Thousand Acres *Jane Smiley* £5.99
- ☐ The Quick *Agnes Rossi* £4.99
- ☐ Tropic of Cancer *Henry Miller* £5.99
- ☐ The Cat Sanctuary *Patrick Gale* £5.99
- ☐ Dreaming in Cuban *Cristina Garcia* £5.99
- ☐ The Golden Notebook *Doris Lessing* £6.99
- ☐ True Believers *Joseph O'Connor* £5.99
- ☐ Bastard Out of Carolina *Dorothy Allison* £5.99

Non-fiction
- ☐ The Proving Grounds *Benedict Allen* £7.99
- ☐ Long Ago in France *M. F. K. Fisher* £5.99
- ☐ The Female Eunuch *Germaine Greer* £5.99
- ☐ C. S. Lewis *A. N. Wilson* £5.99
- ☐ Into the Badlands *John Williams* £5.99
- ☐ Dame Edna Everage *John Lahr* £5.99
- ☐ Number *John McLeish* £5.99
- ☐ Tangier *Iain Finlayson* £7.99

You can buy Flamingo paperbacks at your local bookshop or newsagent. Or you can order them from Fontana Paperbacks, Cash Sales Department, Box 29, Douglas, Isle of Man. Please send a cheque, postal or money order (not currency) worth the purchase price plus 24p per book (maximum postage required is £3.00 for orders within the UK).

NAME (Block letters)_____

ADDRESS_____

_____

_____

While every effort is made to keep prices low, it is sometimes necessary to increase them at short notice. Fontana Paperbacks reserve the right to show new retail prices on covers which may differ from those previously advertised in the text or elsewhere.